Junior Prom

Patricia Aks

SCHOLASTIC INC.
New York Toronto London Auckland Sydney

For Harold, my o.a.o.

Cover Photo by Owen Brown

ISBN 0-590-40970-0

12 11 10 9 8 7 6 5 4   1 2/9

Printed in the U.S.A.   01

Junior Prom

A Wildfire Book

Love Comes to Anne by Lucille S. Warner
I'm Christy by Maud Johnson
That's My Girl by Jill Ross Klevin
Beautiful Girl by Elisabeth Ogilvie
Superflirt by Helen Cavanagh
A Funny Girl Like Me by Jan O'Donnell
Just Sixteen by Terry Morris
Suzy Who? by Winifred Madison
Dreams Can Come True by Jane Claypool Miner
I've Got a Crush on You by Carol Stanley
An April Love Story by Caroline B. Cooney
Dance with Me by Winifred Madison
One Day You'll Go by Sheila Schwartz
Yours Truly, Love, Janie by Ann Reit
The Summer of the Sky-Blue Bikini
    by Jill Ross Klevin
I Want to Be Me by Dorothy Bastien
The Best of Friends by Jill Ross Klevin
The Voices of Julie by Joan Oppenheimer
Second Best by Helen Cavanagh
A Kiss for Tomorrow by Maud Johnson
A Place for Me by Helen Cavanagh
Sixteen Can Be Sweet by Maud Johnson
Take Care of My Girl by Carol Stanley
Lisa by Arlene Hale
Secret Love by Barbara Steiner
Nancy and Nick by Caroline B. Cooney
Wildfire Double Romance by Diane McClure Jones
Senior Class by Jane Claypool Miner
Cindy by Deborah Kent
Too Young to Know by Elisabeth Ogilvie
Saturday Night Date by Maud Johnson
Junior Prom by Patricia Aks

CHAPTER 1 _____

It was the first day of second semester and four of us, my best friend, Mary Jane Gibson (known as M.J.) and my two other closest friends, Terry and Gail, were sitting in a booth at Rico's, sipping Cokes. I joined the collective gloom, bemoaning the fact that Christmas vacation was over. But part of me was pretending, because I really do like school. Of course, I wouldn't admit it.

"We have absolutely nothing to look forward to," Gail complained. Gail always exaggerates and she can make the most ordinary event, like passing the salt, take on an aura of drama. Everything about Gail is dramatic, including her Slavic good looks which are emphasized by her hair held back in a single long braid.

"That was the fastest Christmas vacation I've ever had. Zap, and it was over!" M.J. said, snapping her fingers.

"That's because you're in love," Terry observed. Terry's languid attitude, which matches her willowy figure and catlike green eyes, is misleading, because she has a steel-trap mind. She drives the boys crazy with her seemingly indifferent attitude.

"What does being in love have to do with it?" I asked innocently.

"You'll find out, Amy. And when it happens, it will hit you like a ton of bricks."

"Sure," I said, noncommittally. The problem was I'd already been hit but I couldn't talk about it. You see, I've got this secret crush on Jeff Glasgow, a junior who works at the library, but he doesn't know I'm alive.

"That's how it happened to me. Until I started going with Bud last September, I thought I might have to join a nunnery," M.J. said.

We all burst out laughing, because M.J. looks like a cherub and has a personality that can only be described as merry. She has curly black hair, a radiant smile, and although she's on the short side, a very grown-up figure.

"Anyhow, I'm the only one here — maybe the only tenth-grader in the entire world — who has never had an honest-to-goodness boyfriend," I complained.

"Since I'm just recovering from a broken heart, I'd say you're lucky," Gail said.

"Who is it this time?" Terry asked.

None of us take Gail's broken heart too seriously, because she's always in and out of love. We'd need a score card to keep track.

2

"His name is Joe. He's my brother George's roommate from college. He visited us over vacation and one morning he and I had breakfast together alone, before anyone else was up. I fixed him my specialty, French toast."

"And?" M.J. and I said in a chorus.

"And he told me he wished I was a few years older — that I should wait for him."

"Hardly the basis for a romance, and certainly not for cardiac arrest," Terry observed.

"That's not all," Gail continued. "He asked me a million things about school, and what I liked to do. When George came down to breakfast, the first thing Joe said to him was 'How come you never told me about your sister?' "

"And then what?" I asked.

"And then nothing. The next day Joe and George had to drive back to Hanover, and I was left with a broken heart and nothing to look forward to."

"Knowing you, there'll be somebody new next week. Besides, you can always look forward to spring vacation, and maybe George will bring Joe again."

"Maybe," Gail sighed.

"And then there's always the Junior Prom to look forward to," Terry reminded us.

"The Junior Prom! That's lightyears away," Gail said, and looked at her watch as though that would tell her the exact date of the prom. Then she let out a yelp. "I've got to go pick up my little brother at a birthday party. I promised my mother I'd get there at five o'clock and I've only got ten minutes."

3

"I've got to go, too," I said. "I've got to get things started for dinner tonight, because my mother doesn't get home from her job at the hospital until six."

"I'll walk you to your brother's party," Terry told Gail.

"Great," Gail said. "That'll make both me and Danny happy. He's only seven years old but he has a violent crush on you."

"Shows excellent taste at an early age," Terry said, chuckling.

We had already paid for our drinks at the self-service fountain, so we slid out of the booth, struggled into our parkas, grabbed our canvas bookbags, and left Rico's. It was just beginning to get dark as we stood huddled together in the cold, reluctant to split up.

"Duty calls," Gail announced and she led the way to the corner. Then she and Terry hurried off in one direction, while M.J. and I headed in another. The two of us always walked home together because we live on the same block.

We walked along for at least five minutes without saying a word. I was wrapped up in my thoughts when M.J. said, "I've never seen you so silent. What are you thinking about?"

"You'll laugh if I tell you."

"No I won't, I promise," M.J. said, raising her hand as if she were taking an oath.

"Okay, I believe you. And you promise not to tell anyone, either?"

"Cross my heart," M.J. said.

"Well, the truth is, I'm really worried that

4

I've never had a real boyfriend. I'm sixteen, and although I'm friends with a lot of boys, I've never had a 'one-and-only.' "

"What about Jeff?" M.J. asked. She was the only person in the world who knew I was even remotely interested in him, and I'd sworn her to secrecy.

"I might as well be in love with a Martian for all the attention he gives me. What I mean is I'd like a real relationship — like you and Bud. Do you think I'm normal?"

M.J. stopped walking and stared at me in disbelief. She has a way of smiling with her eyes and then with her lips, so that her whole face lights up. That's the way she looked then, but at least she wasn't laughing. She turned away, shaking her head, and started strolling and talking, almost as though I wasn't there.

"Probably the most normal person I know," she muttered. "Captain of the volley ball team, class reporter for the *Swen*, a terrific student — and pretty besides."

"Who, me?" I asked, knowing I was begging for a compliment.

"Yes, you, dummy. Even my father, who does portrait photography for a hobby, says you have the most expressive brown eyes. He'd love to photograph you some time."

"He said that?" I was really amazed.

"Yep. And you know what I'd give to be built like you. Then I'd be three inches taller, which would make me five-five."

"Sure, but you'd also be flatter. What I

5

wouldn't give to have just a few of your curves."

"Too bad we can't exchange my curves for your inches," M.J. suggested. And then we both laughed.

M.J. has a way of getting me out of my moods, and by the time we reached my house, I had forgotten about my problem. As I started up the path she was saying, "And besides, you have the perfect hair — light brown, and just a slight curl at the end. Mine looks like a black mop by comparison."

"Now I know you're crazy," I said, and waved good-bye.

"Later," she said, and waved back.

As I let myself into the house with my key, I thought how lucky I was to have M.J. for a friend. No matter what bothered me she made me feel better, and for the time being, at least, I stopped worrying about not having a guy.

CHAPTER 2

I guess you could say I'm from a typical suburban family. For one thing, we live in a split-level house in Teaneck, New Jersey. My father drives to work across the George Washington bridge every day to his job in Manhattan, where he is the manager of radio accounts in a medium-sized advertising agency. My mother works three days a week in the administration department of the local hospital.

My parents moved to Teaneck when my brother Greg, who is two years older than I, was ready for kindergarten, so we've lived here almost all my life. One of the reasons they chose Teaneck was that the public schools are so good, and it's close to New York. According to Mumsie, which is what we call my grandmother on my mother's side, my mother made a big mistake not living in New

York City and sending us to private school. I remember once they had a terrific fight about that. I was only eight years old at the time, but I remember every single detail, probably because it's the only time I'd ever seen my mother cry.

My mother had taken me to see the *Nut-cracker Suite* during Christmas vacation and afterward we'd gone to Mumsie's for tea. Mumsie has lived in an apartment hotel on the upper East Side ever since my grandfather died, when I was only two years old. Visiting Mumsie is like going back into the nineteenth century; her building has a doorman and elevator men who still wear white gloves. The furniture is Victorian and so is grandmother. My father, who is generally easygoing and seems to get along with everyone, describes Mumsie as stuffy. My mother defends her, saying she's a woman of principle. What I learned, after that memorable fight, is that my mother is also a woman of principle.

Mumsie believes in private schools, and my mother said that even if she could afford it, she thinks good public schools are better. They went back and forth about this, as though I weren't there, and I concentrated on my pink-iced cupcakes.

"I'm not an elitist," my mother told her.

"You may not be, but that child certainly is," Mumsie said, glancing in my direction.

I didn't know whether "elitist" was something good or bad, but I couldn't wait to get home to look up the meaning.

They continued arguing, but it wasn't until Mumsie made some crack about why hadn't my mother married Philip, who was so rich he didn't have to work a day in his life, that my mother lost her cool.

"Because I didn't love Philip," she said, unable to hold back her tears.

"Love isn't everything." Mumsie sounded so positive.

"To me it is," my mother shot back, quickly recovering. "Love *is* everything." I didn't know it at the time, but I was going to remember that line forever.

Then Mumsie, knowing it was a losing battle, turned to me to ask about the ballet, and then asked if I wanted to take ballet lessons. She seemed disappointed when I told her no, but at least she didn't give me an argument.

The truth is I'm crazy about Mumsie, even though I know she's a snob. She makes me feel special and says I'm her favorite grandchild (she has no use for boys). She has always spoiled me, buying me things I don't even need. My mother used to argue with her about that, but now she's given up. Besides, my mother has told me that she knows I'm more sensible than Mumsie and that I would never be ridiculously extravagant the way Mumsie is. Naturally, after my mother said that I felt I had to live up to my reputation, and I bend over backwards not to let Mumsie go berserk when she takes me on one of her shopping sprees.

I suppose one of the reasons I've always gotten along with my mother is that she trusts me. And she's not bossy, like most of my friends' mothers.

CHAPTER 3 ——————————————

I suppose the other thing that makes us a "typical" suburban family is that I have a "typical" kid brother. Kenny's in the sixth grade, has carrot-colored hair which he inherited from Mumsie, a zillion freckles, and is a nonstop talker. He's also very demanding. As soon as I opened the door, I could hear him bounding down the stairs, yelling, "What took you so long? I can't figure out my math homework and you know they won't let me watch TV until my homework's done. I can't believe we get homework the first day after vacation. Where have you been?"

"Hi," I said, hanging my parka in the hall closet, shoving my book bag in the corner of the closet, and ignoring his plea. My aim in life is to calm him down. My parents say I have the best influence on him. He can be a real pain, but I have to admit he's cute.

"Hi," he said, standing on one foot in front of me and waving his algebra book in my face.

"You're going to have to wait," I said firmly. "We have to get dinner ready because mother doesn't get home until six tonight. You set the table and I'll heat up the stew and fix the salad."

"And then you'll show me how to do just two problems? I think I've figured out most of them."

"Okay, okay." He followed me into the kitchen. "Where's Greg now?" I asked him.

"He's practicing with his group at Teddy's house."

"No wonder it's so quiet."

"Yeah, and he gets away with murder. We do all the work around here and he'll drop around in time to eat," Kenny complained as he opened a kitchen cabinet.

"Don't worry," I assured him. "He'll be in charge of clean-up."

I added some wine and a little water to the stew and put it on the low burner. Next I fixed the salad while Kenny finished setting the table. Then he plopped himself down on a chair in the kitchen, his algebra book flung open on the table, and pleaded, "Just show me what x is."

I looked at the problem, scribbled down some calculations, and quickly solved it. "You're brilliant!" he exclaimed.

"Thanks. But it won't do you one bit of good if you don't figure out the process. Look at everything that leads to the answer."

"Sure, sure. Now do the last one."

"Nope, you're on your own now."

"You're tough," he mumbled, knowing I wouldn't give in, but out of the corner of my eye I could see he had started figuring out the answer.

I had almost finished mixing the oil and vinegar and adding condiments to the salad when he let out a shriek. "Eureka!" he shouted, and leapt up from the table. "I'm a genius!"

"Is that the thanks I get?" I asked.

"I couldn't have done it without you," he said, giving me his chipmunk grin and backing out of the kitchen.

A minute later my mother let herself in the kitchen through the back door and gave me a peck on the cheek, saying "Hi, sweetie. I see you've got everything started. The stew smells delicious." She walked through the kitchen, muttering, "I don't know what I'd do without you, Amy."

"What about me?" I heard Kenny gripe. "I set the table."

"You're wonderful," my mother said. "If it weren't for you kids we wouldn't be eating for hours."

Then I heard Greg burst in the front door. "Hi, everyone. Sorry I'm late, but the group was just grooving on a new arrangement and we couldn't break up. Can't interrupt the creative juices, you know."

"Sure," Kenny said. "Amy and I are the slaves around here."

"Don't worry, kid. I'll be on clean-up." He stuck his head in the kitchen, where I was washing my hands over the sink. "Deal, Aim? You won't have to lift a finger the rest of the night."

"Deal," I answered, drying my hands on a paper towel. "It's a good thing, too, because I haven't touched my homework."

"No library today? Why not?" he asked.

"Easing myself into the routine after the holiday. You know how it is."

"Do I ever," Kenny piped up as I brushed past him in the hall to get my book bag from the closet.

Then I trudged up the stairs to my room. It isn't too large but it has everything I need. It looks like a sitting room because I have a hi-rise instead of twin beds, which would take up too much space. And I can still pull out the bottom bed and have an overnight guest.

I was hoping to get my homework started before dinner, but I'd just sat down at my desk when I heard my father's voice. My father is really a lot of fun, but he does have a thing about having meals on time. He claims it's a hang-up from his childhood, when his mother was so lackadaisical about meals that lunch would be ready so late it turned into dinner. He promised himself he'd never let that happen to his kids.

I went downstairs to say hello to my father, who was in the kitchen taking a bottle of beer out of the fridge. "Hello, Amy," he said, pushing the refrigerator door shut with his elbow and pulling me toward him with the arm that was holding the beer bottle. "Now I've got my two favorite things," he said, laughing, and hugged me. My father always makes me feel terrific, as though I'm the most important person in the world. When he's around, everything seems more fun.

When we sat down at the table, everyone seemed in a particularly good mood. Yet, for some reason I didn't understand, I felt out of it. Everyone was talking so much that no one noticed I was unusually quiet. I was glad that Greg had volunteered to clean up, so all I did was clear the table and then I escaped to my room.

CHAPTER 4 ———————————

When I got upstairs I sat down at my desk, pulled out my French book, and idly turned to the French idioms that I was supposed to memorize. But I couldn't concentrate. I tried to figure out what was bothering me. It certainly didn't have to do with my family, because although I have occasional run-ins with my brothers about work around the house, that wasn't the case tonight. The fact is I seem to get along better with my family than anyone else I know. Last semester I learned that was true for sure.

It was the beginning of the school year and we had a new English teacher, Ms. Newman. One of her first assignments was for each member of the class to describe his or her family and compare it to an idealized one. She promised the papers would be confidential, but I personally thought she was snooping into our private lives.

Actually, everyone I talked to liked the assignment. It gave them a chance to get down in black and white what really bothered them. And Ms. Newman was true to her word — she never revealed what was in our papers. She did discuss in general terms how everyone had complaints about parents who didn't understand him or her, or were too strict, or disinterested, or always in a bad mood. Then she said there was only one person whose real family seemed to approximate that person's ideal family.

I knew she was talking about my paper, and I stared straight ahead, trying to keep my face like a sphinx, so no one would notice me. It wasn't that I was embarrassed by what I'd written, but I didn't want to come across as a Goody Two Shoes. I suppose that's one of my main problems, that I want to seem like everyone else.

Later I confided to M.J. that Ms. Newman had been talking about me and I hoped no one knew it. M.J. assured me that I didn't have to worry, and I should be glad I didn't have a mother like hers who was constantly picking on her.

"I guess I don't want to seem different from everybody else," I explained.

"You're not different," M.J. insisted. "Just lucky."

"I know that," I said. "I just want to *seem* like everybody else."

"You're not the only one," M.J. reassured me.

That made me feel better, but still I was convinced that I suffered from a severe case of wanting to conform, and my condition was not improving. Now, as I sat at my desk thinking about my need to be like everyone else, I couldn't help remembering the conversation that day at Rico's — everyone I knew but me had now, or in the past, a boyfriend.

I thought about Jeff, but I couldn't entertain the remotest idea of getting involved with him. He was just too unreachable, and I didn't want to get hurt. Besides, for all I knew he already had a girlfriend. But the more I thought about him, the more I realized he fulfilled my dreams.

Since he is a junior we never have classes together, and the only time I see him is in the library when I take books out. Even so, I've memorized his face. There's nothing special about his looks, but I think he's really cute. He's average height, on the skinny side, wears wire-rimmed glasses that magnify his large brown eyes, and has unruly brown hair that he can't keep off his forehead.

Actually, I spend a lot of time in the library, but it has nothing to do with Jeff. It's the one place in the world I have peace and quiet, and I seem to get my homework done in half the time. Also, I love to read and I'm always taking out books.

At home there are so many distractions — Greg is either practicing with his group in the family room or listening to the stereo at full volume. If he isn't begging me to help him with his homework, Kenny is running around like a maniac with one of his friends. Or else one of my friends calls on the phone and I can never resist talking. So it's very logical that I should stay in the library.

Of course, a fringe benefit of working there is that I get to see Jeff. But we never have very lengthy conversations and they're never personal. When he stamps my books, he invariably makes some remark about what I'm taking out. I think he must have read everything in the library.

Before Christmas vacation I'd assembled a pile of books, everything from Hemingway's *The Sun Also Rises* and Fitzgerald's *The Great Gatsby* to *The Hobbit* by Tolkien. As he concentrated on stamping, he remarked, "You have the same taste that I have in books."

If he'd made a declaration of love, I couldn't have been more flustered. "We do?" I said, idiotically.

He looked at me with a shy grin, but neither of us could think of anything to say. I started frantically stuffing the books in my canvas bag, as though my life depended on it. I seemed to be all thumbs and I hoped he didn't notice. I didn't have to worry; two squealing third-graders had shoved some books on the counter, and I could see out of the corner of my eye that he had turned his full attention to them. I floated all the way home, repeating to myself, *You have the same taste that I have in books.* I knew it was ridiculous to attach so much importance to such an innocent statement, but I couldn't get it out of my mind.

I have a cuckoo clock in my room, and I was startled when the cuckoo sang out nine times. I couldn't believe I'd daydreamed so long and hadn't even begun to study. It's time, I said to myself, to stop thinking about love and concentrate on my French. Madame Dumas, our French teacher, is a bustling little round lady who has taught at our school for such a long time that she is practically an institution. She doesn't miss a trick behind her old-fashioned spectacles. She advised us to say the idioms so that we'd get accustomed to hearing ourselves speak French, as well as helping us memorize them.

I started reciting the first one aloud. Then I glanced at the second and third, and let out a groan. It seemed as though the world was conspiring against me — all the idioms were about love. That made sense, because Madame Dumas teaches conversational French in clusters. One assignment will focus on dining and food, another on taking a trip, and still another on shopping. Those were certainly innocent enough subjects, none of which would trigger an emotional response, but it was just my luck that this assignment would turn my mind to mush. The first two almost made me dissolve:

A quoi ça sert, l'amour?   What good is love?

C'est triste et merveilleux   It's sad and marvelous.

It took an enormous act of will to actually learn the French and pull myself out of what was practically a romantic swoon. When I'd finally committed the idioms more or less to memory, and stopped interpreting them in relation to myself, I was relieved to turn to my science book. The chapter we were assigned was on cloning. That, for sure, was an unromantic subject. But the whole topic of love and boys was not one that would stay submerged for long.

My friends and I once decided that the longest we could ever go without discussing boys was ten minutes and that would only happen if we took a vow of silence. I had always thought that I had a lot of self-discipline when it came to thinking about romance, but in the next couple of months the whole idea of boys was to become an obsession.

CHAPTER 5 ⸻

The obsession began in the middle of March at Rico's.

It's understood that every Friday afternoon M.J., Terry, Gail, and I meet at Rico's. (School lets out an hour early on Friday; no extra-curricular activities are scheduled, and even the library is closed.) Whoever gets there first saves a booth. Otherwise, we hang out at the fountain, but that means we have to put a lid on some of our private conversations.

There's an unwritten law that if one of us has something "better to do," which is a euphemism for having a date, we don't have to make any explanations if we don't show. But even Gail, who is the most boy-crazy of us, admits that rapping with us is a lot more fun than having a Coke with a nerd you can't even talk to. M.J., of course, would like to spend all her free time with Bud, but Friday afternoons he works for his father, who is a pharmacologist and owns his own drugstore. Bud either works behind the counter or makes deliveries. M.J., who always sees the bright side of life, says there are three advantages to Bud's working: one, he makes some extra change; two, her mother can't bug M.J. about spending *all* her time with one person; and three, she loves being with her girl friends. We all agree that our Friday afternoon sessions are special because they're For Women Only.

On this particular Friday, Gail was the first to arrive and had managed to save us a booth. As soon as the rest of us showed up, dumped our bags on the floor, and settled down at the table, she brought up the subject that would take over my life.

It started innocently enough, with Gail saying that the previous day there had been a meeting of the Whirls. The Whirls is the high school's social committee, which plans and promotes all the social activities throughout the school year. It has members from each class, and Gail is one of the three tenth-grade representatives.

"You guys are going to have to help me," Gail began. "This is going to be *the* event of the year."

"You say that about every event," Terry pointed out.

"I know," Gail acknowledged, "but this really is going to be the greatest."

"What is it?" I asked.

"It's still pretty far off, but we want to

23

get an early start so everything will be perfect."

"I can't stand the suspense," M.J. said. "Tell us!"

"The Junior Prom," Gail announced proudly, as though she'd invented the idea.

"But it's not till May," Terry said.

"The last Saturday in May, to be exact," Gail said.

"Isn't your enthusiasm a little premature?" Terry asked.

"Not really," Gail replied, ignoring Terry's sarcasm. "It's less than three months off."

"But it's only for juniors," I said. "Where does that leave us?"

"It is for juniors," Gail explained, "but that doesn't mean sophomores can't go if they're invited by a junior. M.J. certainly doesn't have to worry."

"That's right!" M.J. said, beaming. "Bud *is* a junior and I never knew until this very moment what an advantage that was."

"Well, I don't think any of us have to worry," Gail said. "We all know juniors."

"We may all *know* juniors, but that doesn't necessarily mean we'll get invited to their prom," I pointed out.

"It only takes one invitation," Terry said.

"I suppose," I replied, as nonchalantly as possible. Actually, I thought Terry had nothing to worry about. She was being pursued by several juniors who would probably cross swords to determine who would take her to the prom. I, on the other hand, couldn't think of a single eleventh-grade boy who might ask me.

As though Gail was reading my thoughts, she said, "I don't know who I'm going with, either. But Tim Durwood is head of the JP committee and I think he's terrific — six feet, blue eyes, blond hair. He looks like some kind of Greek god. I'm hoping to make an impression on him at the next meeting."

"With your good looks?" Terry asked.

"With my efficiency," Gail lied, half-smiling.

Then we all laughed because Gail was so transparent.

I thought of the juniors I knew, and although I worked with a few of them on the *Swen* — which is n-e-w-s spelled backwards — and we all got along, it was strictly a business arrangement. Of course, Jeff came to mind, but that was a one-way street — me, going his way. The last time I got two words out of him was a week ago at the library.

He sort of gave me a compliment, although it was nothing personal. I had written an article for the Pro and Con column on the editorial page. The column presents both sides of current issues that are controversial, and last week's discussion was on "Nukes Versus No Nukes." Since I feel so strongly about No Nukes, it was an article I had no trouble writing. First I wrote a general paragraph about why nuclear expansion is destructive in every sense of the word. Then I listed specifics, such as the possibility of accidents that cause radioactive steam and gas to seep into the atmosphere (I used Three Mile Island as an example). Then I wrote about the problem of disposing of radioactive waste and the enormous cost of construction. Finally, I pointed out the alternative ways of providing energy — coal, wood, solar, wind.

The day my editorial appeared, a million people told me how much they liked it. It seemed to me that everyone in our school was anti-nukes. But the comment I treasured the most was Jeff's.

I bumped into him on the way to the back of the library, where I usually do my homework. His arms were loaded with books, and as he brushed by me he said, "That was a good editorial you wrote."

"Thanks," I said, slowing down, hoping he would say something else. My eyes followed him, but he was so intent on returning the books to their proper place that he didn't even notice I was standing there.

As Gail went on about how she was going to trap Tim, I thought about who I might work on. But I drew a blank.

On the way home from Rico's I told M.J. my fears about not getting an invitation.

"A zillion things can happen between now and May," she said. "Who knows, maybe you'll meet your one-and-only — who happens to be a junior — tomorrow."

"You are the eternal optimist," I observed.

"Besides," M.J. added, "you can't start worrying about it now. It's much too early."

"You're absolutely right," I agreed, and I made up my mind to put thoughts about the prom on the back burner.

But no matter how hard I tried, they wouldn't stay there. Besides, ever since the Whirls meeting to plan the prom, that's all anyone seemed to talk about. I still tried to appear indifferent, but the truth was I cared — desperately.

Terry, whom we call our class psychiatrist because she's very honest and intuitive and doesn't ever say anything just because she thinks we might want to hear it, says that there are three steps one should follow in handling a problem. The first is to face it head-on; the second is to attack it; and the third step — if the problem is unsolvable — is to live with it.

I'd already faced the problem: I needed someone to take me to the prom. Now I was ready to attack it. I wasn't sure what form that would take, but the following Monday I discovered, without quite knowing how it happened, that I was launching my campaign!

CHAPTER 6 _____

I was sitting alone in the back of the library reviewing my notes for a history test that was scheduled for the next day. The tables are usually empty after school because everyone tears out of the building as soon as the final bell rings. Therefore I was surprised to see Grant Dorsett settle his lanky six-foot frame opposite me. I knew who he was because, although still a junior, he was the school's star basketball player, and also, by general consensus, the best-looking. For once, the cliché "tall, dark, and handsome" made sense. Grant had straight black hair, dark green eyes, and the kind of skin that always seemed tan, even on the grayest day of winter. It was hard not to stare at him.

Of course, I didn't expect him to know me, so I was amazed when he said, "Hi. You're Amy Ross, aren't you?"

I gulped and said in astonishment, "Yes, how'd you know?"

"The column on 'Nukes Versus No Nukes' was the basis for a whole discussion in our Soc class. You didn't know you were famous." He gave me a wry smile.

"But how did you recognize me?"

"We kept quoting your editorial, and after class someone pointed you out to me in the hall."

"You're kidding," I said, suddenly feeling very self-conscious.

He didn't seem to notice and went right on talking. "My name's Grant Dorsett."

"I know."

"How do you know me?" he asked.

I couldn't tell if he was putting me on or not. "You're famous, too," I said grinning.

"I know," he admitted and shrugged his shoulders. "What can we do about all this publicity?"

"It's not easy," I said.

"Well, frankly, if I don't settle down and do my English assignment, I'll be infamous. Mrs. Jenner, who happens to be one of my fans, gave me a ten-day extension on a paper so I could practice for last Saturday's game. The paper's due tomorrow and I haven't even started. Incidentally, did you see the game?"

"I know you won," I said hedging.

"That's not what I asked."

"No, I didn't see it but I heard you scored the winning basket in the last few seconds of play." Thank goodness, I thought, that Greg had mentioned the game one night at dinner. At the time I wasn't even interested.

"It was exciting, probably one of the best games I've ever played," Grant admitted, not exactly immodestly.

"Sorry I missed it," I said. Actually, I couldn't care less about basketball, but for the purposes of this conversation I really was sorry I missed it.

"But I've got to stop thinking about basketball and write this paper."

"And I've got to finish my homework."

We both turned back to our books and concentrated on studying for at least fifteen minutes. Then Grant sighed so loudly that I couldn't help but look up.

"This is hopeless," he complained. "I just can't seem to get started."

I noticed he had *The Great Gatsby* in front of him and had been jotting down notes.

"I just finished reading that myself," I said. "It's terrific."

"How come you had to read it? It's not on the tenth-grade reading list."

"Ever hear of reading for pleasure?"

"Might ruin my shooting arm," he answered, and gave me that funny half-smile.

"What's your paper on?" I asked.

"I have to write an in-depth analysis of one of the characters — not Gatsby. We already talked about him so much in class that there's nothing left to say."

"I bet you chose Daisy."

"You're right!" he said so loudly that I started to giggle, and he clapped his hand over his mouth in embarrassment. Fortunately, there was no one sitting near us, but we *were* in the library and there were SILENCE PLEASE signs all over the place.

"She should be fun to write about," I said when I finally managed to stop laughing.

"For somebody who can write easily. It's not my specialty," Grant groaned.

"Hey, maybe I can help," I offered, hoping I didn't sound patronizing.

"Would you?" he yelped. "You might just save my life."

"Sure," I nodded. "I just read it over Christmas vacation so it's still clear in my mind."

"Wow," he said admiringly. "I can't imagine spending any part of my vacation reading."

"But I love to read," I explained. "You don't know what you're missing."

Grant looked at me very hard for a few seconds and then said, "I think you mean it. Maybe I am missing something."

"Anyhow, the library closes soon so we better get started."

"Right," he agreed. "Just tell me how to begin."

"Well, when I was in the seventh grade I had an English teacher who said you always need a 'hook' for a story. I've never forgotten that, and it works, too."

"The only 'hook' I know is a hook shot in basketball."

"What's that?" I asked.

"That's when you stand sideways to the basket and toss the ball over your head with the hand furthest away from the basket," he explained. "I can't see what a hook has to do with my paper."

"Same thing, in a way. You've got to have an angle."

"Like what?"

"Like what is Daisy's most outstanding characteristic?"

While Grant frowned and chewed on his pencil, I couldn't help thinking how cute he was. And the fact that he was a junior — and a possible candidate for escorting me to the prom — flashed through my mind. I had a brief fantasy about dancing with him at the party of the year but was jarred back to reality when he said, "She's spoiled rotten."

"Who?" I asked stupidly.

"Daisy, who else?"

"Oh yes. That's exactly right. She's spoiled and self-indulgent and only cares about having a good time."

"Now how do I get two pages out of that? It seems you've summed the whole thing up in one sentence."

"All you do is find something in the story that proves your point. You elaborate on that, and you can quote from the book directly."

Grant had earmarked a number of places

in the book and thumbed through them intently, his forehead creased in worry. Suddenly he stopped frowning and his face lit up. "You mean like what she says after she has her baby girl, 'I hope she'll be a fool — that's the best thing a girl can be in this world, a beautiful little fool'?"

"You got it," I said. "And you can also say how other people see her. There's a really good description at the end of the book. I'll show you." I reached for his paperback copy, which was so mangled I was afraid to turn the pages for fear they'd drop out. I thumbed through it gingerly, and Grant said, smiling, "Don't worry. Nothing more can happen to that copy. I already dropped it in the bathtub."

I resisted saying that's no way to treat great literature, but instead I just chuckled. He might be a cultural cretin, but he was a junior and very good-looking. I wouldn't want him to hold it against me that my knowledge of basketball was zilch, so why should I blame him for not liking books?

"Here's the place I mean," I pointed out excitedly. "It's page 180, where the narrator, Nick, describes Daisy and her husband, Tom. 'They smashed up things and creatures and then retreated back into their money or their vast carelessness, or whatever it was that kept them together, and let other people clean up the mess they had made.'"

"That really sums her up perfectly," Grant

said. "Also, in the beginning she's described as the most popular young girl in Louisville. She dressed in white and had a little white roadster, and a million young officers were constantly asking her out." He was very pleased with himself.

"See, I said, "it's not so hard to write a paper once you get the knack."

"I never thought so before," he said happily. "You really should be an English teacher."

I wasn't sure if that was a compliment or not.

"Listen," Grant said, "I owe you a favor for getting me started on this. I hate to cut the lesson short, but the library is about to close. How about giving me lesson number two this Saturday night?"

"Are you asking me out?" I asked coyly, hoping I didn't show how excited I was.

"You really are smart," he said, half-smiling.

"I'd love to see you Saturday," I agreed. "And we can talk about your favorite subject — basketball."

"Nope," he protested. "I'm beginning to think maybe that's not the most interesting topic in the world."

Of course, I didn't take him seriously. Grant Dorsett was known as Mr. B. He'd been on the varsity team since tenth grade, which was very unusual, and there was no doubt that he'd be elected captain of the team next year.

I knew nothing about basketball, but I had five days to bone up on the subject. The next day I would get some books out of the library and start memorizing. After all, Grant wouldn't stay interested in me for long if I couldn't talk to him at all about his favorite thing in life.

CHAPTER 7 _____

When I got home, my mother was in the kitchen basting a roast chicken. It was one of her early days at the hospital, so she had plenty of time to cook, which she says is "pure pleasure" for her. There were two kinds of pies cooling on the windowsill.

"Smells delicious," I said, poking my head through the kitchen door. I still had on my parka, and my book bag was slung over my shoulder.

"Hi, sweetie," she said, closing the oven door and glancing at me over her shoulder. Then she added, "You're glowing. Tell me what happened."

The problem with my mother is that I couldn't keep a secret from her even if I wanted to. She always knows what kind of mood I'm in. Fortunately, she's tactful enough not to quiz me when I'm down, even though she notices. I guess she thinks it's okay to ask me how I am when I'm up, and then I'm not too reluctant to answer.

"Grant Dorsett asked me out for Saturday," I told her.

"That's nice," she said, taking off her apron and hanging it on a wall hook. "Who's he?"

"Oh mother," I groaned, "he only happens to be the school's star basketball player, even though he's still a junior."

"That's nice," she repeated. "Now get ready for dinner. We'll be sitting down in about ten minutes. Daddy's already in the den, having a beer. And the boys are upstairs, getting washed, I hope."

"Okay, mom. I'll get ready." I backed out of her way. Then I flew upstairs because I couldn't wait to tell Greg about Grant.

I dumped my things on my bed and then banged on his door. He was just coming out of the bathroom, which is in the hall, blotting his face with a towel. He must have dunked his head under the faucet because his dark hair, which my father says is on the long side for a senior who plans to be accepted at "the college of his choice," and which Greg claims is unusually short for a lead guitarist in a rock band, was dripping all over the floor.

"Here I am, Amy. What's up?"

"Grant Dorsett asked me out. Can you believe it?"

"No, frankly." His brown eyes crinkled in a smile. "What possessed him?"

"Thanks a lot," I said sarcastically.

"What are you going to talk about?" he asked.

"That's a problem." I was serious.

"Only kidding," he said, rubbing his head vigorously. "You're never at a loss for words."

"I might be this time, I'm afraid. I don't know a thing about basketball. Maybe you can tell me a few things."

"Sure," Greg said. "You see, there's this little basket, and this big ball, and the point is to drop the ball in the basket. Whichever team does it the most times wins."

"You're a big help," I groaned, but I couldn't keep a straight face.

"I know about basketball," Kenny piped up. Kenny is like an elf who appears unexpectedly and no one knows how he got there or where he came from. Now he was standing directly behind me.

"Tell me everything you know," I said.

"The main way to get around the court is by dribbling." Kenny explained it so seriously that I couldn't tell him that was the only thing I did know.

"What's that?" I asked, playing dumb.

"That's what babies do when they eat pabulum," Greg said.

"Shut up, Greg," Kenny barked. "I'm trying to teach Amy something."

"I appreciate it, too," I said.

"Hey," I'll show you," he squealed, and sped down the hall into his room, which is next to Greg's. He reappeared in a flash, bouncing a tennis ball in front of him, moving rapidly forward at the same time.

"See," he said, glancing up at me and Greg. "This is dribbling."

"Excellent," Greg graded him. "You should be a coach."

Kenny ignored him, dribbled his way into the bathroom, and shut the door. Then I went into my room, which is smaller than the boys' but has its own bathroom. My hi-rise has a red and white checked spread, and I have a red corduroy chair with a standing lamp beside it. The rest of the furniture is built in, which saves space, and the wall over my desk is lined with books.

I went into the bathroom and washed my hands. Then I ran a comb through my hair, thinking about how Greg would never take me seriously about wanting to learn about basketball and I'd just have to find another source of information. It would be a little embarrassing to explain why I had this sudden impulse to learn everything I could about a sport that never interested me before. I decided to lay off the subject with my family and do some research on my own.

That, however, turned out to be futile. The minute we sat down at the dinner table, Kenny said, "I taught Amy about dribbling."

My father and mother looked at him as though he was crazy and said in a chorus, "Dribbling!"

Then Kenny blurted out the fact that this

guy Grant Dorsett, the best basketball player in the school, had asked me out, and I didn't know what to talk about and the least he could do after all the times I'd helped him with his homework was teach me about the game.

Everyone laughed, but I thought that if I ever wanted to keep something secret, Kenny was the last person in the world to let in on it. Of course the real reason I wanted to impress Grant was so he'd stay interested in me long enough to see me through the prom. Fortunately Kenny didn't know that or he would have made a public announcement; Greg would never stop teasing me; my mother would worry because I cared so much; and my father would make light of a situation that to me was deadly serious.

"I'm sure he didn't ask you out because of your knowledge about basketball," my mother said.

"That's right," my father agreed. "Sometimes these things backfire."

"What do you mean?" I couldn't help asking, even though I wanted to get off the subject.

"Well," my father explained, "Bill Jenkins, my roommate in college, went with a girl one summer. She apparently was so anxious to impress him that when she found out he was on the ski team, she pretended she loved skiing too. That was okay through the summer and fall, but after the first decent snowfall, Bill invited her to go on a skiing weekend.

Of course she couldn't say no. You know the rest of the story."

"You mean she wasn't any good," Kenny observed.

"Not only wasn't she any good, she'd never been on skis before. And as it turned out, she had no natural aptitude."

"Did they break up because of that?" Greg asked.

"I don't know if that was the reason, but the romance didn't survive the winter. I'm sure it wasn't because of her athletic ability. More likely it had something to do with her character."

"You mean she was deceptive," my mother said.

"Exactly. You see, it never pays to not be yourself." My father was wrestling with a chicken bone and he didn't seem to be directing his conversation at me.

Besides, I wasn't pretending to be something I'm not. Maybe I would switch from volleyball to basketball, since every six weeks in gym we were given a chance to change our team sport. That wasn't being deceptive. I'd just be picking up a new interest.

CHAPTER 8 _____

That evening after I'd helped with the dishes I bolted upstairs and called M.J. More than anything, I've wanted a telephone in my room, but my parents consider that an "unnecessary extravagance," so they compromised and I have the next best thing — a phone in the hall with an extension cord that slides under the door. I can actually close the door and have some privacy.

I stretched out on my bed and dialed. As soon as M.J. picked up the phone, I told her about Grant.

"Terrific," she squealed. "Now your JP problem is solved."

"Not quite," I said. "So far all he's done is ask me out for this Saturday. The prom is more than two months away."

"I think you'll make it till May," she assured me.

"Not if I don't learn something about basketball," I lamented.

"What's that got to do with it?" M.J. asked.

"Everything," I answered.

"I don't know," she said slowly. "Seems to me that's not why he asked you out."

"You sound like my mother!" I said, genuinely amazed.

"But it's true," M.J. insisted. "You obviously didn't talk about basketball *before* he asked you out."

"That's true," I said.

"So what did you talk about?"

"As a matter of fact, we talked about one of my favorite subjects — books. To be more specific, *The Great Gatsby*."

"How'd that ever happen?"

"He was in the library struggling with a paper and I volunteered to help him."

"See. He was into your subject. Why don't you keep it that way?"

"That was only today, M.J. He couldn't care less about books. In fact, he was amazed I'd read anything that wasn't assigned. I know he won't like me if he thinks all I do is study."

"You'd never come across like that. I personally think you shouldn't pretend to be a dumb jock when you're not."

"M.J.," I wailed, "you, of all people, should understand. He's a junior, remember, and cute, and a star. I can bend a little if it means getting asked to the prom."

"I suppose," M.J. mumbled, but I knew she wasn't convinced I was doing the right thing.

"Have you finished your French?" I asked, abruptly changing the subject.

"Haven't even started."

"Me neither," I said.

"We better hang up. I'll call you if I get stuck."

"And vice-versa."

"Incidentally, if you want to be really up on basketball, why don't you read the sports page?" M.J. suggested.

"Great idea! I knew you'd see it my way."

"Not exactly. But you are my best friend and I'll do what I can to help you."

"Thanks," I said. "I'd appreciate that. But do me one favor and don't tell anyone about my campaign."

" 'Course not. I just hope it works."

"It better," I said. *Tempus fugit.*"

"You mean *temps vole.*"

"However you say it, time is running out."

As soon as I put down the receiver, I got up from the bed and went into the hall to look for the paper. The morning paper is supposed to be left on the hall table so that it's available to everyone. The paper comes in four sections and by the time each member of the family gets his or her hands on it, it's a mess. Even Kenny looks at the paper now, because he has a social science teacher who insists that his class keep up on current events. When Kenny is done with it, it's in a shambles, but fortunately it had been left on the hall table and the sports section was intact.

I grabbed it, returned to my room, and quickly scanned the pages for anything I could find on basketball. There was an interview with Willis Reed, a former Knick star and coach. He talked about how he was going to join St. John's University as an assistant coach, where he'd be working with Lou Carnesecca. Then there was a quote that I thought I should remember: "Basketball is in my blood. I have been around the sport since I was thirteen years old, and I don't think of anything else in the world than getting back into the sport." The article said Reed was named the N.B.A. rookie of the year after the 1964–65 season. By the time of his retirement in 1975, he had become the first player to be named the most valuable player in the league All-Star Game. He became the Knick coach for the 1977–78 season but was dismissed because he was too outspoken and stubborn for management.

That was a lot of information, but it was only the beginning. Luckily, I've got a good memory and that's one of the reasons I've always had an easy time getting good grades. It never occurred to me that I would be using my quick study ability to get a guy. I still had five days, counting Saturday, to assemble more information, and I was pretty confident I could learn more than enough to get me through our Saturday night date. And maybe I'd have a little left over for the next time — if, as I fervently hoped, there was a next time.

CHAPTER 9 _____

The next day, as soon as the final bell rang, I hurried to the library and went directly to the sports section. There was a whole shelf on basketball, and I picked out three books that I was sure would make me reasonably knowledgeable, if not an expert. I took them to the back of the library where I usually sit. Even though I was going to take them home and knew I should tackle my homework first, I couldn't resist looking at one of them. First I turned to *The Fundamentals of Basketball*. It was a short book, and it didn't take me long to skim it. I concentrated so hard on learning the basic shots — the layup, the hook, the jump, and the overhead set shot — that I didn't notice Jeff was at the next table until I heard a book slam shut. It sounded like a bullet in the silence of the library.

I looked up and noticed he was replacing old

takeout cards with new ones. The process involved removing the old card by slipping a knife under it, spreading rubber cement on the new card, placing it on the inside cover, and then firmly closing the book to make sure it held. If I hadn't known better, I would have thought he was making noise in order to get my attention.

He glanced at me sideways and said, "Sorry. I didn't mean to disturb you."

"That's okay," I said. I wasn't sure why but I hoped he wouldn't notice what I was reading.

"This is really a bore," he groaned.

"What are you doing?" I asked, as if I didn't know. But I didn't want the conversation to end.

"Replacing the old, used-up takeout cards with new ones."

"Who's up front?"

"Ms. Kruger, the head librarian, is at the desk so I'm free to do this manual labor."

He smiled shyly, and that had the peculiar effect of making me lose the power of speech. In desperation, I turned back to reading about the jump shot.

I hadn't even finished the first page when Jeff said, "That must be really good."

Here it comes, I thought. No way of avoiding letting him know what I'm reading.

"Sort of," I muttered.

"What's the name of it?"

"*The Fundamentals of Basketball*," I said in a monotone.

"Really," he said, as though he couldn't quite believe it. Then he quickly added, "You must be doing an interview for the paper."

"Not exactly," I said. "It's just something I want to find out about."

"Sure," he said, without expression.

I felt stupid, but Jeff was the last person in the world I could tell my reason for reading about basketball. To avoid further questions I concentrated on my reading — at least I pretended to. The words didn't make too much sense anymore. I was relieved when Jeff gathered up the books he'd been working on and went to the front of the library.

There were only about forty minutes left until the library closed, so I decided to do my history assignment. At least I'd get that out of the way before I got home.

I hoped that Mrs. Kruger would still be at the front desk when I checked out the basketball books, but no such luck. Jeff had taken over, so as nonchalantly as possible I shoved the books toward him. He stamped the first one and didn't say anything. After he read the title of the second, *How to Win at Basketball*, he looked at me quizzically but still remained silent. When he came to the third, *Everything You Wanted to Know about Basketball*, he just shook his head as though I had flipped out. He hadn't given me the opportunity to say anything, even defensively, so I just picked up my things and muttered "See ya," as I turned away.

When I got home, I yelled hello to everyone

in the kitchen and then rushed upstairs, dumped the books in my room, closed the door, and slowly made my way downstairs. My father was making his specialty — shish kebab — and Kenny was helping put the meat, onions, mushrooms, and tomatoes on skewers.

"Hi, Amy," my father said. "I thought I saw something flash by a minute ago. What's the big hurry?"

"Nature called," I lied.

"Hope you made it," Kenny said, pointing a skewer at me as though it were a fencing sword.

For some reason I wasn't in the mood for messing around with Kenny, so I ignored him and started setting the table. A few minutes later my mother and Greg came in the back door.

"We got a gig, we got a gig," Greg shouted. "Two weeks from Friday at a Sweet Sixteen party in Tenafly."

"That's great," my father said. "Maybe all this rehearsing will pay off."

"It's about time," my mother said. "Don't you think so, Amy?"

"It's terrific," I said, faking enthusiasm. I *was* really happy for Greg, and everyone was in a good mood. I couldn't figure out why I wasn't with it. After all, I'd gotten an unexpected high mark on my math test only because we were marked on a sliding scale; the editor of the newspaper had come up to me during lunch and asked me to think up another Pro and Con column; and I had a super date for Saturday night. It didn't make sense that I wasn't feeling happy, with all these good things happening. But deep down, I knew I was suffering from what Terry would describe as a severe case of *angst*, which means anxiety — and that's a lot harder to get rid of than a bad cold!

CHAPTER 10 _____

By the time Saturday arrived, I was so well versed in basketball that I could have gone on a quiz show with confidence. I knew enough about the subject to get me through a million dates. I'd even gone to the trouble of reading all the sports sections in the past issues of the *Swen*. If need be, I could tell you the names, positions, and abilities of all the important players in our school as well as in the major leagues. I was bubbling over with information. But if ever Robert Burns's lines, "The best-laid schemes o' mice an' men gang aft a-gley," applied, it was on Saturday.

Grant called me around ten o'clock in the morning to say he'd pick me up at six; we'd go to Woody Allen's latest movie and afterwards wind up at The Disco. The Disco is actually a loft over an office building. It's furnished with round wooden tables of various sizes and lit with hurricane lamps, which gives it a romantic look. The main attractions are the spacious dance floor, which is in the center of everything, and the music, which is provided by tape. No hard liquor is allowed, but beer is sold, and hamburgers, and all the junk food you can imagine. It's the "in" place, and I was really excited that we were going there.

"Terrific," I said.

"Incidentally, we're going with Billie Casper and his date, Hilary Starr. You know them?"

"I know who they are. Billie's the best forward on the team."

"That's right." Grant sounded surprised. "How'd ya know that if you never see any of the games?"

"I have my ways," I replied mysteriously. "And everyone knows who Hilary is." Hilary is a junior, blond and beautiful, and has a reputation for being a snob. She's in all the school plays, and even though the lead in the spring musical usually goes to a senior, she managed to beat out the competition for the starring role in *Brigadoon*, which goes on at the end of the school year.

"Billie was able to get his family's car for tonight," Grant told me. "We'll pick you up at six."

"I'll be ready," I said.

I had just hung up when the phone rang again. This time it was Terry, who didn't bother to say hello. "I just spoke to M.J.," she said. "Today is the perfect day to get Gail's birthday present. She told me that her entire family is going to Brewster, New York, for the day for some sort of family celebration. We'll pick you up on the way to the shopping mall. What time do you want to get started?"

"Soon as possible," I answered.

"Have to get home to prepare for the big date," Terry teased. By this time, of course, my close friends knew I was going out with Grant, but only M.J. knew I'd been preparing for it all week.

"Let's just get started," I said. "In fact, why don't we eat at the Fountain?"

"Good idea," Terry agreed. "I'll call M.J. back, and we'll pick you up in an hour. Meanwhile, thing up something we can get Gail."

"I'll work on it," I said, and hung up.

Whenever Terry, Gail, M.J., or I have a birthday, the other three always try to dream up an original present. We keep outdoing ourselves with unique ideas. My birthday was in June, and even though my parents gave me some super presents, including a clock radio, my favorite was the huge fish bowl that my friends gave me, decorated with colorful pebbles, miniature bushes, and four turtles. Each turtle had a different name painted on it — Gail, Terry, M.J., and Amy. So far, they're all still alive, but if anything should happen to one of them I plan to replace it. That way, their gift will be in perpetuity, which is the same as saying it will go on forever. It really was the greatest present ever, and it would be impossible to top it.

Terry and M.J. were on time, and as we strolled over to the mall, the first thing Terry said was, "I suppose you've been practicing your shots all morning."

I glanced at M.J. suspiciously, but she raised her eyebrows and shrugged her shoulders.

"Why would I have to do that?" I was trying to sound innocent.

"Only kidding," Terry said, and I realized that M.J. would never break a confidence. I knew I was getting much too sensitive about this whole thing with Grant and would have to handle it better.

"What'll we get Gail?" M.J. asked.

"There's a big department store in Texas that sells His and Hers elephants," Terry said.

"How about a scarf made of ostrich feathers?" I suggested.

By the time we arrived at the Fountain, we were outdoing each other with wild suggestions. After we settled into a booth and gave our order for an oversized pizza and Cokes, I said, "Let's get serious. Since Gail is always in love, we should get something with hearts."

"That's a neat idea," M.J. agreed. "At least that narrows the field."

"Good thinking," Terry approved. "We'll wander around and see if something with hearts will hit us."

After we polished off the pizza and paid the bill, we left the Fountain and window-shopped our way across the mall. We lingered at the jewelry store window, quickly passed an elaborate hardware store, and then stopped dead in our tracks at the Bath Shop. We all started yelling at once, for there, heaven-sent, was the perfect gift for Gail. It was a white hamper, covered with red hearts, and a wastebasket to match. "Perfect!" "Irresistible!" "Fantastic!" we shouted.

Even though it was over our budget, we decided to plunge and buy both items. While we waited for them to be gift-wrapped, I thought philosophically, why can't all problems be so simple? For a while I'd been momentarily distracted thinking about and finding Gail's birthday present, but my anxieties didn't stay submerged for long. I couldn't stop wondering if I'd make a good impression on Grant. Would he like me well enough to ask me out again? Would our relationship last until that crucial date in May?

'Hey," M.J. whispered, putting her hand on my shoulder, "you can come back to the real world now. Mission accomplished."

I guess it was pretty obvious that I'd been a million miles away. "What mission?" I asked.

M.J. looked at me as though I was demented and said slowly, "Birthday present, for Gail. Remember?"

"Sure," I said, and chuckled. "And Terry is paying." Terry was in line at the cashier's desk.

M.J. smiled at me, and then glanced at her

watch. "It's only two o'clock. Let's check out the record store."

"You're on," I agreed, thinking I'd better do something for the next few hours or I'd really get myself into an extreme state of nerves. After all, I kept telling myself, it's only a date. But deep down I knew it was much more than that . . . It could mean getting asked to the Junior Prom.

CHAPTER 11 ——————————

The evening started off all wrong, mainly because of Hilary who definitely thinks she's the greatest invention since sliced bread. I mean she's a snob with a capital S, and if she's not talking about herself she's either brushing her hair or looking in the mirror. As soon as I climbed in the back seat of the car with Grant and exchanged hi's with everyone, she started in.

"I hear this isn't one of Woody's best," she began, "but my coach tells me I can learn even from a poor vehicle."

"Vehicle," Grant kidded her. "You make it sound like we're going to see an automobile show."

She ignored him and proceeded to turn the mirror above the windshield toward her.

"Hey," Billie complained, "I need that to drive *this* vehicle."

"Don't get so excited," Hilary snapped, fluffing her hair with her hand. "I just wanted to see if everything was perfect."

"Speaking of perfect," Grant said, turning to me, "for the first time in my academic career, I got an A on an English assignment."

"You mean Mrs. Jenner liked your *Great Gatsby* paper?" I asked.

"Thanks to you." Grant squeezed my shoulder and kissed me quickly on the cheek. "She said it was the best I'd ever done. Will you give me some coaching the next time?"

"Sure," I said, thinking that I didn't want him to like me just for that reason.

"We're reading Hemingway now and I know we'll have a written assignment. Do you suppose I should use the same approach?"

"Well," I said thoughtfully, "every paper requires a different approach. As in basketball, the backboards vary from court to court, in material, in resilience, in size." I thought I was being clever getting that information across, but Grant ignored what I said.

"Hemingway is my kind of writer," he went on. "He gets right to the point."

"You mean he would go for the clean shot rather than the bank shot?"

"Huh?" Grant mumbled, as though he didn't know what I was talking about, but we had arrived at the movie house and didn't continue the conversation.

Billie parked the car, we got out, and Hilary drawled, "We're here. Let's hope it's not too painful."

"I always love Woody," Grant said.

"Me too," I agreed.

"He does have a cult of admirers," Hilary acknowledged. "But they don't necessarily know anything about theater."

I thought of several possible put-downs but figured it was a waste of time. After all, the only person I was interested in was Grant.

We couldn't get seats together, and Hilary insisted that she wanted to sit up front on the aisle. As she drifted toward the first three rows, Grant guided me to a couple of seats in the rear.

"She's something else," Grant whispered in my ear, when we settled down. Actually, I was relieved that I wouldn't have to hear her snide remarks during the movie, but I didn't tell Grant that. All I said was, "Alone at last." Grant chuckled, and then as soon as the lights dimmed, he held my hand. He didn't let go until the movie was over, and I figured he must like me a little, and not just because he needed my help in English. But even though I liked Grant, I couldn't help thinking about Jeff while we watched the screen. I would have liked to be holding Jeff's hand, but I knew he wasn't interested in me that way. I tried to keep him out of my mind, but it wasn't easy.

As we waited for Hilary and Billie outside the movie house, both Grant and I agreed that Woody was funny as ever. We were cracking up as we talked about some of the scenes, and then Hilary approached us with

Billie trailing. She raised her eyebrows when she saw us laughing and said, "That entire film was a series of one-liners. You call that acting?"

"We thought it was a lot of fun," Grant told her.

"What's wrong with one-liners, if they're original?" I asked.

Hilary just shook her head, as though the question weren't worth answering. Then she turned to Billie and muttered under her breath, "amateurs."

Billie didn't seem to want to get embroiled in any controversial discussion and said, "Let's walk to The Disco. It's only a few blocks from here and I won't have to park again."

"Good thinking," Grant said, grabbing my hand and leading the way. We walked quickly and I huddled close to Grant in order to avoid the buffeting wind.

It didn't take long to reach the loft, and Grant held the elevator for Billie and Hilary. Hilary, as soon as she entered the elevator, pulled a brush out of her bag and started brushing her hair.

"I don't know why we had to walk in this weather," she complained. "Now my hair's a mess."

"I think it looks good," Billie consoled her.

"You may like the Diane Keaton type, but personally I think her looks as well as her acting leave something to be desired."

The elevator had arrived, the door opened, and there was a blast of music that was so loud Billie was spared having to defend himself. Strobe lights were flashing, and you could almost feel the electricity in the air.

We hung our parkas on the coat rack that lined the wall and headed for a table. So much was going on at once that I wondered if I could remember my basketball "homework." And even if I did, how would I get it across to Grant, especially if Hilary was sitting there, talking about nothing but herself? Surprisingly, Hilary was going to give me just the opening I was looking for.

There were some really good dancers on the floor, and Billie made the mistake of commenting on one girl who looked as though the gold metallic jumpsuit she was wearing had been molded over her body. Her black hair was flying as she gyrated with the music. The fact that she had a partner was unimportant, because all eyes were on her.

"She's something else," Billie observed. We all knew who he was talking about.

"Sensational," Grant agreed.

"I have to admit you're right. I think I could learn to hate her," I kidded.

Hilary, who had been gazing at herself in a hand mirror, managed to look up long enough to see who we were talking about.

"No taste," she remarked. It wasn't easy to tell if she was talking about the metallic flash or our opinions.

Billie, whose role seemed to be to keep the peace, stood up and said to Hilary, "Let's show them how it's done."

As they headed for the dance floor, Grant leaned toward me and said, "Hilary's got to be the most competitive woman I've ever seen."

"She's another Bill Russell," I remarked.

"What are you talking about?"

"I'm talking about competition. Did you know that Wilt Chamberlain, when he played for the Philadelphia Warriors in 1965, negotiated the biggest salary ever? It was for a $100,000."

"So what?" Grant was frowning.

"Bill Russell, who was playing for the Boston Celtics, had this incredibly bitter rivalry going with Wilt the Stilt, and he negotiated a contract for $100,001. Can you imagine grown men acting that way?"

"That is pretty childish," Grant acknowledged. "But we didn't come here to talk about basketball contracts. Let's dance."

"Sure," I said, getting up from the table, thinking what a master I was at talking his language. It wasn't going to take me long, however, to be reminded of one of Burns's other lines:

"Oh wad some power the giftie gie us
To see oursel's as others see us."

CHAPTER 12————————————

About once an hour at The Disco, the management turns off the taped music for ten minutes or so. That gives the customers a chance to order drinks and food at the self-service bar. During one of these intervals we had returned to our table, and Hilary, before she sat down, said, "I'm famished, Billie. Let's get something to eat."

"Fine," Billie said. "I'll take orders."

"Coke for me," I told him.

"Make it two," said Grant. "We'll settle the financial damage later."

I watched Billie weave his way to the service bar with Hilary close behind. "Billie looks like he's threading a needle right to the basket," I commented.

"Hey," Grant said thoughtfully, "I thought I heard volleyball was your game and that you're captain of the girls' team."

"Oh that, actually I'm thinking of switching my team sport to basketball." I tried to sound offhand.

"Really?" Grant seemed surprised. "You'd never catch me switching to volleyball."

"I like experimenting," I said defensively, but what I was thinking was that *he* wasn't trying to impress *me*.

"Besides," Grant said, "I'm hoping to get a basketball scholarship."

"That's terrific. Maybe you should look into St. John's. Willis Reed, a former Knick coach, is there now. He's working with Lou Carnesecca, who's supposed to be the best there is."

"You're a regular *Who's Who in Basketball*," Grant exclaimed.

I was spared having to think of a reply to that remark, because someone clapped her hands over my eyes and squeaked, "Guess who?"

"M.J.," I shouted. "I'd know that voice anywhere."

"Brilliant deduction," she said, and we all laughed as M.J. and Bud sat down at our table.

Bud and M.J. are exact physical opposites. Bud's at least a head taller than M.J. and has straight light brown hair, but they look really cute together. And they get along better than any couple I know.

"Isn't this place great when the music stops," Bud observed. "Then we can hear ourselves think."

"You sound just like my father," M.J. giggled.

At that moment Hilary and Billie, carrying a tray, returned to our table. They said hello to M.J. and Bud. Then Bud jumped up.

"Oh, oh, we better move," Bud said, pulling M.J. by the hand. "We'll probably never see you again in this crowd. But don't forget next Saturday. There's going to be a pep rally at the gym for the basketball team, and afterwards Alan is inviting the team and their dates to a little party at his house. It'll be on the quiet side compared to this, but at least we'll be able to find each other."

As they disappeared into the crowd I glanced at Grant, but he was busy taking the Cokes off the tray and didn't look at me. Now I had a new worry. I knew there was going to be a pep rally, and because of my new interest I planned to attend, but I had no idea there was going to be a party afterwards. Alan, the basketball coach, has a reputation for being big on morale. His way of bringing the team together is to have get-togethers socially, usually a week or two before a big game. The guys on the team, the bench-warmers, and the cheerleaders all bring dates, but since I've never been especially friendly with any basketball players, I'd never been to one of these booster parties. M.J. had been to a couple because of Bud, who's a sub, and she said they were a lot of fun.

Now I wondered if Grant would ask me to go with him to Alan's. So far he hadn't even mentioned the pep rally. Was he avoiding the subject because he didn't want to get involved with me? Maybe he'd already invited some other girl. Was this evening a trial run, and if I passed he'd invite me? There were so many questions whirling in my head that I didn't know what to think about first.

I decided to play it cool, at least until we were on the way home. If I was lucky, Grant would save me the necessity of bringing up the subject and just come out and ask me. If that didn't happen, I'd figure some way to bring it into the conversation.

The rest of the evening I continued to let him know that I knew the names of players on the major leagues, the best way to stop the pivot man, the real meaning of aggressive defense, and on and on. I tried to be as subtle as possible, but one time when the music had stopped and we were alone for a few minutes at our table, I noticed his eyes wandering over the crowd. I was going on about Bob Cousy, who although only six feet one and 185 pounds, was an outstanding All-America player in college and became famous for the "behind-the-back" dribble. I was scoring points like crazy, I thought but suddenly Grant jumped up and said, "Excuse me a second. I'll be right back."

My eyes followed him as he bolted toward the opposite side of the room and then stopped cold in front of a girl with long, auburn-colored hair. She was alone, for the moment, probably because she'd just come from the

Ladies' Room. She was Deborah Dunston, the most glamourous girl in the junior class. Greg had told me that she'd been going with Tom Bennett, the senior class president, but that they recently split up. It was natural that Grant would move in on her. But where did that leave me?

He seemed to be whispering something in her ear, and then I could see the two of them laughing. As he backed away, I was sure I could see his hand, which had been resting on her shoulder, slide down her arm as though he were reluctant to leave her.

When he returned to the table, he slid into his chair and said, "Sorry, there was someone I had to say hello to."

"That's okay." I spoke tonelessly, and concentrated on sipping my Coke.

I suddenly felt frozen and was actually glad when Hilary suggested we leave before the music started up again.

"I have an early morning voice lesson," she explained, "and this smoke-filled room is terrible for me."

"Your wish is my command," Billie said amiably. "But what about you two?"

"I'm ready to split," Grant said, a little too eagerly.

"Me too," I muttered.

"Let's move it," Grant urged, getting up. He actually held my chair as though he wanted to make sure I wouldn't hold things up.

We got our coats and headed for the car.

Even though Grant took my arm, I knew it wasn't because he liked me, but because he wanted to make sure I didn't lag behind.

The air was icy, not unlike my mood, and we hurried toward the car in silence. When we had piled in, I still didn't feel like talking. It didn't matter, because Hilary was going on and on about how ridiculous it was to have a car and not park it a reasonable distance from one's destination.

"Might as well go by bus," she snapped.

"Fresh air never hurt anyone," Grant said. "Right, Amy?"

"Right," I mumbled, aware that his usual good spirits seemed better than ever.

Billie pulled the car up to my house and turned around to face Grant. "Take your time," he said. "I'll take Hilary home and come back for you."

"That's not necessary," Grant said quickly.

Obviously, I thought, he wasn't interested in spending much more time with me, or even giving me a good-night kiss.

He held the door for me and I scrambled out, thinking that there wasn't much time, I may never have an opportunity again, so I might as well hint about Alan's party.

When we got to my house I pulled the key out of my pocket and slowly opened the door. As I walked into our center hall, I said as casually as possible. "You going to the pep rally next Saturday?"

"Of course," he answered, as though the

question were crazy. "Alan wouldn't let me miss it if I wanted to."

I hoped he would say something else, like ask me if I were going, but nothing happened.

"Well, thanks for tonight," I said after a long pause.

"Sure thing," he said.

I was facing him, holding on to the door and hoping he'd at least give me a kiss on the cheek. But all he did was back away, saying, "Take it easy, Amy," and I watched him disappear into the darkness.

CHAPTER 13 ───────────

As I lay in bed that night, I thought about the evening. Obviously, I'd blown it. I wasn't sure how, but I knew that I could scratch Grant off my list of possibilities. He hadn't even bothered to ask me if I was going to the pep rally, so that certainly finished it for Alan's party, to say nothing of the prom.

Well, I comforted myself, I hardly knew Grant until a week ago, and I wasn't about to let him ruin my life. With that thought in mind, I buried my head in my pillow and promptly fell asleep.

I slept late and when I finally woke up it was already past eleven. I took a quick shower, put on my most disreputable jeans — which are also my favorite — and a plaid flannel shirt I inherited from Greg when it shrank in the laundry. Old clothes always make me feel good, and I was determined not to let my zip score with Grant get me down.

He's not the last junior in the world, I told myself, and I didn't even like him that much.

We always have brunch on Sunday, and by the time I got downstairs everyone was bustling around the kitchen. My father was making his "thin as a dime" pancakes, Kenny was stirring scrambled eggs in a double boiler, Greg was working on the bacon, and my mother was fixing a bowl of mixed fruit.

"Morning, princess," my father said, flipping a pancake in the air. "Just in time for the Sunday special."

"You look none the worse for wear," Greg said, appraising me from top to toe. "How was it?"

"Not exactly cosmic," I answered honestly, hoping he wouldn't continue the questioning.

"Where'd ya go?" Kenny asked.

"First to the Woody Allen flick, and then to The Disco."

"You dribble around the dance floor?" Kenny started laughing so hard at his joke that I didn't have to answer.

Then my father said, "C'mon gang, let's get synchronized. I have a batch of pancakes ready and they're only good when they're hot. Get me a platter, Amy."

I handed him a serving dish from the cupboard, and Kenny squealed, "I need one too, Amy. Hurry up, before these eggs geal."

"Con-geal," Greg said patronizingly.

"Whatever it is, if we don't eat them soon they'll taste like glue."

I helped him dish out the eggs, and Greg,

who had meticulously pressed the bacon between paper towels, now put it on the same platter. When everything had been brought into the dining room, we sat down. Greg helped himself to a large stack of pancakes and started wolfing them own.

"You don't have to pig out," my father warned him.

Greg smiled sheepishly and slowed down. Then, in order to take the attention off himself, he turned to me. "Tell us the gory details about last night, Amy. Did Grant show you his spectacular moves?"

"It was very crowded at The Disco and we didn't stay that long," I told him, avoiding talking about Grant.

My mother, who sensed that I didn't want to be quizzed, said, "Who wants to go to Englishtown with me? There's a flea market that's open today and they have terrific buys."

My mother's an antique freak, and I think some of her enthusiasm has rubbed off on me.

"Not me," Kenny piped up. "Scott's coming over and we're going to work on our model planes."

"I'm rehearsing, of course," Greg said.

"How about you, Aim?" my mother asked. "I know Daddy isn't interested."

"Love it," I answered, glad that I had something to do out of the house.

"Terrific. We'll leave as soon as we clean up the dishes."

"I owe you one, Amy, so you and Mom can hit the road as soon as you finish eating."

"Gee, thanks, Greg," I said appreciatively.

"And Kenny will help, of course," Greg added.

"Why is it always me?" Kenny griped.

"Because you're so good at it," Greg joked.

Before Kenny boiled over, my father said, "Listen, Kenny, I'm going to help too. We able-bodied men will get everything done in a flash while the womenfolk spend their time in frivolity."

"You menfolk are wonderful," my mother said, and even though it seemed to me they'd been married for centuries, she gave my father — as they say in the old-fashioned novels — an adoring look.

After we polished off the Sunday brunch specialties, my mother said to me in a stage whisper, "Let's make a quick getaway before they change their minds."

"Good thinking. I'll meet you in the garage in five minutes." I pushed my chair back from the table.

I flew up the stairs and quickly washed my hands and ran a comb through my hair. I couldn't help thinking how lucky I was to have such a super family. The problem was, no matter how much they might distract me, I couldn't stop thinking that what I really needed was a guy — by necessity a junior; hopefully not a wimp, a nerd, or an airhead; and obviously someone who would ask me to accompany him to a particular function occurring on the last Saturday in May.

CHAPTER 14 _____

I had a great time with my mother at Englishtown, and she tactfully didn't mention Grant or ask a million questions about what happened. We wandered around all the booths and I fell in love with a miniature pink lustre tea set that cost three allowances. My mother loved it just as much as I did. Then she told me that she'd actually invited Mumsie along. Mumsie had said she didn't want to make the trip but insisted that my mother "buy something for my favorite grandchild and don't worry about the cost." I had to laugh when I heard that, and my mother teased me about my "expensive tastes," which had skipped a generation.

"This is adorable," my mother remarked, picking up the tiny teapot.

"I love it," I said wistfully.

"It's yours!" my mother exclaimed, and told the rumpled old man behind the booth to wrap it carefully.

"I love it, I love it," I raved, and wondered for the moment if I really was like Mumsie, who firmly believed that the only way to get out of a bad mood was to buy something. For the moment, at least, I thought she was right.

I fell asleep in the car on the way home, and by the time we arrived at our house, my bad vibes about the previous evening had practically disappeared. In fact, I had myself convinced that everything had happened for the best. I no longer had to brief myself on current happenings in a sport that didn't remotely interest me; I could get back to reading for pleasure instead of spending my spare time ingesting facts and figures that would show how "interested" I was in someone else's sport; and now I didn't have to go to the pep rally.

With a certain amount of glee, I stuffed the basketball books into my canvas bag. I couldn't wait to get them out of my sight forever! Then I called M.J. and told her exactly what had happened. I confided to her that I really wasn't unhappy about losing Grant — whom I never had actually won — but that I had to get an invitation to the prom. M.J. reassured me that there were plenty of juniors left who weren't attached, and that something was bound to happen in the next few weeks.

I wasn't looking forward to the next day at school when I'd still have to field questions from Terry and Gail. As it happened, I bumped into Terry in the corridor after the first bell rang and we were rushing in opposite directions. "How'd it go?" she asked.

I pointed my thumbs down and Terry just shrugged her shoulders and gave me a "so what" look. I can always count on Terry not to overreact.

That wasn't the case with Gail, who sits next to me in math. She's probably the most outspoken person I know, and I should have been prepared for her barrage of questions: "Where'd ya go? Who was there? Did he ask you out again? Are you going to see him at the rally? What about the prom?"

I answered her in monosyllables, and when it finally dawned on her that the evening was a downer and I wasn't even going out with Grant again, she looked genuinely dismayed.

"I'm sorry," she apologized. "I feel so rotten for asking so many dumb questions. Why didn't you just tell me to shut up?"

"It's okay," I said. "I've already recovered."

"That's terrific. Besides, you shouldn't be wasting your time on a dumb jock. Meanwhile, I'm still working on Tim."

"And?"

"And nothing."

"There's still plenty of time," I said, trying to make myself feel better, as well as Gail.

"Sure," she answered, without her usual enthusiasm, and I realized I wasn't the only one who had worries.

CHAPTER 15 _____

That day while I was standing in line at the cafeteria for lunch, Bob Gilman, the editor of the *Swen*, came charging up to me. Bob is short, wears horn-rimmed glasses, has traces of acne, and is a human dynamo. He's not exactly the romantic type but he is kind of wonderful, and I was particularly flattered when he said to me, completely disregarding the fact that we weren't exactly alone, "We've decided what we should do with you."

"What?" I asked, totally bewildered.

"We're doing a whole feature on music, and we want you to write something. We're putting the Pro and Con column on hold."

"That's great," I said, "but I'm holding up the line. Can't I talk to you about this later?"

"I don't have time later. I'm sitting over there." He pointed to a table at the far end of the room. "Come over and I'll tell you the whole story in two seconds. Deal?" His impatience was overwhelming, and I could understand why some people couldn't stand him even though he did get things done.

"Deal," I told him, sliding my tray along and feeling very pleased that he'd sought me out.

I took my tray to the table where my friends were sitting, hastily told them I'd be right back, and then rushed over to where Bob was sitting with the managing editor, Barbara Gleason. Barbara is a female version of Bob, but a head taller. Together, they put out the best *Swen* editions the school has ever seen.

"He found you," Barbara observed, not bothering to say hello and chewing on an apple.

There was an empty chair next to Bob and I sat down.

Bob got right to the point. "What we're doing is running a series of in-depth articles on music of the sixties up to the present. It will include separate stories on the Beatles, hard rock, surf rock, right through to new wave." Having said that, he took a large bite out of his tunafish sandwich.

"What do you want me to write?" I asked.

"We're giving you the plum," Barbara answered. "We want you to do an interview with Len Altman. I suppose you know who Lenny is."

"That's great," I exclaimed, ignoring her sarcasm. Everyone knew Len Altman. He was the lead guitarist in the school band, and actually had his own groupies — mostly seventh- and eighth-graders. I, of course, wasn't one of them, but you couldn't be a student in our school and not know who Len was.

"When do I meet him?" I asked.

"We'll set up a meeting and let you know. And of course you'll get a by-line." Bob was devouring the rest of his sandwich in seconds.

"Terrific," I said.

"We'll check with you later," Barbara added, indicating that I was being dismissed.

"See ya," I said, and floated back to my table where Gail, Terry, and M.J. were seated.

"What was that all about?" M.J. asked.

"I'm going to do an interview with Len Altman for the *Swen*."

"Fantastic," M.J. shouted.

"Wow," Terry muttered, obviously impressed, but typically not showing any emotion.

"What an opportunity," Gail exclaimed. Then she added thoughtfully, "You know he's a junior."

"I know," I acknowledged. "So what?"

"So isn't that what we're looking for?"

"I never even thought of that," I said honestly. I realized then that I was so excited about the prospect of doing an interview with a by-line that nothing else mattered for the moment.

"Where are your priorities?" Gail chuckled. I knew she was half-kidding, but my heady mood started to fade.

"I know my priorities," I replied seriously, "but Lenny and me? Ridiculous."

"Nothing ventured, nothing gained," Terry commented.

"But he's a star," I said. "He wouldn't be interested in me." Somewhere, I knew I was begging for reassurance, and M.J. didn't fail me.

"Every star needs an astronomer. How else can it be identified?" she said.

"You mean me?" I asked.

"Just go up to him and say, '*You* star, *me* astronomer,'" Gail quipped, improvising on the "Me, Tarzan, you Jane" routine.

Then we all cracked up, but the truth was, Gail had started me thinking. After all, Lenny was a junior; I would have him all to myself for an interview; and who knows what might happen? The thought that he might get around to asking me to the prom was unbelievable, but now I couldn't stop thinking about it.

I knew Bob Gilman would set up our meeting soon, and meanwhile I had to find out something about rock. If I came across as a musical retard, Len certainly wouldn't be interested. As usual, I decided the best place to get information was through books. I couldn't wait until school was over and I could get to the library!

CHAPTER 16 ─────

As soon as the last bell rang, I raced to the library. The first thing I did was unload my basketball books. It was like shedding a skin. I must have been smiling to myself because Jeff, who had just approached the front desk, looked at the books I had returned and said, "You look happy. Is that because you've mastered the art of basketball?"

"Not exactly," I replied.

"If you really like sports books, you should read the new Reggie Jackson biography. He's one of the greatest ballplayers of the century but also a very complicated person. This book makes him real, not just a cardboard hero."

"I don't care much about baseball," I blurted out.

"But you do care about learning how to play basketball?" He shook his head in bewilderment.

I thought, What I really care about is you,

but you only think of me as a bookworm. I said aloud, trying to keep him interested, "Maybe I should read about Reggie."

"Not if you don't want to." He sounded cool.

I couldn't think of anything else to say, and besides, some kids were clamoring behind me. I stepped out of the way and decided to concentrate on my new project.

I hurried to the music shelf and spent the next thirty minutes picking out books on music since the sixties and on rock guitar. Since we can only take out four books, I had to be very selective.

Although I was anxious to start reading them immediately, I forced myself to do my math assignment first. That was always a hassle, but I managed to finish it before the library closed.

Jeff was at the front desk when I went to check out my books. This time I was ready when he remarked, "Looks like you're doing a paper on rock guitar."

"Nope," I said, as casually as possible. "I'm doing an interview with Len Altman for the *Swen*."

"That's great," he commented. "But from the looks of these titles, it seems as though he's going to interview you, instead of the other way around."

"Well," I defended myself, "I think I should know something about the subject."

"Probably," Jeff said, obviously unconvinced.

Neither of us spoke as Jeff stamped each book with a date, and I shoved them in my canvas bag. As he handed me the last one, he looked at me intently through his wire-framed glasses, which magnified his deep brown eyes, and said, "I just read Kurt Vonnegut's book, *Jailbird*. It had me laughing out loud. All about a bag lady who's a million-aire. You should read it."

"I'd like to," I said, "but I just don't have time now."

"You don't have time for good literature any more?" He gave me a raised-eyebrow look.

"Maybe when I finish the interview. You know I like good books."

"Sure," he muttered, and abruptly turned away, busying himself with some papers that were sprawled over the desk.

"See ya," I said, and headed for the door.

"Later," he mumbled.

The day was darkening as I walked home and I was suddenly feeling very strange — still excited about the prospect of interview-ing Len, but aware that I was being deceptive. I would have loved to read the Vonnegut, especially because Jeff recommended it. But I didn't really have time. Or did I? I always had time in the past for good books. Well, I had the rest of my life for that. The main thing now was to get through the interview, and in the process get Len Altman interested in me long enough to last through May.

I mapped out my strategy. Not only would I

read up on the historic aspects of rock and guitar, but also I'd scan the papers for reviews about current rock concerts. And although I'd never been into guitar playing, I thought now would be the perfect time to take Greg up on his offer to teach me a few chords.

As soon as I got home I went to Greg's room, where I found him actually doing his homework and not strumming on his guitar. He seemed grateful for the interruption, so I plunged right in and told him that I had an interview coming up with Len Altman.

"You seem to be majoring in stars these day," he kidded me. "First Grant and now Len."

"It's only an interview, not a date," I said modestly, not daring to mention that getting Len to ask me out was my most devout wish. "But I need your help."

"I know," he groaned, "you want me to teach you everything there is to know about guitar in one easy lesson."

"You got it!"

"I'll do anything to avoid doing homework," he said, getting up from his desk.

He picked up his guitar which was leaning against the bed and started strumming it. I watched him with new eyes, for the first time aware of how adept he was in handling the instrument.

"You're good," I exclaimed, as though I had never heard him play before.

"Flattery will get you everywhere."

"I mean it, Greg."

"You act as though this were a new experience for you."

"I always took your playing for granted. Anyhow, show me how, please. It's crucial to my future. I'll be ruined if you don't help me."

"Never let it be said that I was responsible for that," he said. Then he got up and I watched as he scrounged around in the back of his closet, and backed out with an old guitar, muttering, "The things I have to do . . ."

He dusted off the old guitar with a dirty T-shirt that happened to be lying on the floor. Then he tightened the strings and tuned it.

"Sit there," he ordered, pointing to the bed and handing me the guitar. Then he pulled up his desk chair opposite me, saying, "Just try and follow what I do. I'll go slow."

I carefully watched the way he wrapped his fingers around the neck of the guitar with his left hand and started strumming the strings with his right. I tried to imitate him exactly, but my fingers wouldn't bend right and my strumming sounded like squeaks.

"I'm hopeless," I wailed.

"Anybody can learn a few chords," he sighed. Then he actually reached over and pressed my fingers down on certain strings. "Now strum," he instructed, "and you'll have an A chord."

I did what he said and to my amazement played something that sounded like an honest-to-goodness A chord.

Greg smiled his approval, and then placed

85

my fingers on some other strings. "Strum that and you've got a D chord."

I did what he said, successfully, and then he told me to go back to the A.

"But I've already forgotten that," I complained. "Maybe I'm a musical retard, for real."

"Probably," Greg agreed. "But you haven't scratched the surface." Then he frowned, and slapped his head. "I've got my first *Learn-the-Guitar* book, and if you do what it says, even you can play a few songs!"

He got up and reached for a pile of music books that were on the top of his book shelf. "Haven't looked at these in years," he said, picking up the T-shirt and dusting them off.

"Did you learn by reading these?" I asked.

"I may have looked at them in my early childhood. Of course, with my natural aptitude, I didn't stick with them for long."

"But you think they might help me?" I asked anxiously.

"There's a slim chance," he said, pulling one of the books out of the pile. "This one. called *How to Play the Guitar*, has a subtitle: *Beginning Lessons for Children 10 and Up*."

"I think I've been insulted."

"It's nothing personal. A beginner's a beginner. But one thing you have to do is trim your nails."

"You're kidding, I hope. I've finally got them where I want them." My fingernails weren't very long, but they were just right, and perfectly even.

"For the sake of art, my dear," Greg said imperiously. "And you do want to impress Len."

"I didn't say that," I protested. "I just want to get a better understanding of what it's all about."

"Sure," Greg said, a smirk on his face.

I could have killed him then, but decided I needed his help and I better not let him bug me.

Just then Kenny bounced into the room. "Dinner is practically ready," he announced. "Hurry up."

"Relief at last," Greg sighed.

"Listen, if it's too much trouble . . ." I started to say.

"Only kidding," Greg said. "What you should do next is follow the lessons in the book. They really are helpful. And if you get stuck, call on me."

"Thanks," I said, somewhat mollified.

"Now take the guitar, study the book, and practice, practice, practice."

"Okay," I sighed. I took the guitar and the music book and headed for my room. As I dumped them on my bed I thought, I have a long way to go; but I felt good that I was making a beginning.

CHAPTER 17 _____

A s soon as the kitchen had been cleaned up, I went directly to my room, anxious to resume my guitar program. I was debating whether to practice playing the chords or start reading on the subject when the phone rang. Then Kenny banged on my door, shouting, "It's for you, Amy. Some guy."

I've tried to train Kenny not to make remarks like that, because the person on the other end of the line might hear them, but it's a lost cause. Kenny will never learn!

The phone call turned into a bombshell, because it was Bob Gilman who told me, breathlessly, "It's all set up. Your interview with Len is right after school tomorrow in the music room."

"Oh no," I mumbled. "That's much too soon."

"Too soon?" Bob screeched. "I practically killed myself getting him to agree to see you tomorrow. He said it was the only time he had all week."

"Yeah, but I don't know anything about guitar."

"You don't have to. All you have to do is ask questions."

"I guess so," I mumbled, thinking I could never explain to Bob that I didn't want to come across as a musical moron — which had nothing to do with the interview but had everything to do with getting Len interested in me.

"Listen," Bob said impatiently, "if you don't want to do the interview, just tell me. I'll get someone else in two seconds."

"Of course I want to do it," I replied, slightly panicky. "I'll be in the music room as soon as school lets out."

"Good," he said, and hung up before I even got a chance to ask him what kind of questions I should ask Len.

I slowly put down the receiver, drifted back to my room, closed the door, and stood like a stone staring at the guitar and the music books. Even if I stayed up all night reading and trying to nail down a few chords, the situation was hopeless. I wouldn't absorb enough information to make an impact on a flea. I might as well cross Len off my list of potentials.

Now, at least, I could watch a little TV and make some brownies, which I almost never have time to do.

After I'd watched TV and had called M.J.

to fill her in on the latest events in my life, I wandered into the kitchen. I was mixing the ingredients for the brownies when Greg came into the kitchen, looking for something to eat. It was less than two hours after we'd had dinner, but Greg is a bottomless pit.

"Glad to see you're making some brownies," he remarked, "but why aren't you practicing?"

"The interview's tomorrow, and there's not enough time for me to learn anything."

"Probably better that way," he said, peeling a banana. "You'll come across as a sweet innocent of the music world."

"Shut up," I snapped. He'd hit a nerve, because that's exactly what I was afraid of — coming across as a "sweet innocent."

"Hey, take it easy, Aim," Greg said. "You're much too uptight about this whole thing."

"I know," I apologized. I knew I was being ridiculously tense.

"To tell the truth, if you have to 'wing it' in the interview, you might come up with something really fresh."

"Like what?"

"Like . . . I don't know. That's why it'll sound original."

"I hope you're right, Greg." I went to turn on the oven.

"Look, you're a good writer and it's easy for you to talk to people. That's why you were chosen to do the interview in the first place. What else do you want?"

I was thinking, What I want right now, more than anything in the world, is to have Len invite me to the Junior Prom. But all I said was, "I just want to ask the right questions."

"Stop worrying, will you? You'll do fine. For all my wise advice, can I lick the bowl?"

"That's the least I can do for you," I said, pouring the brownie mixture into a baking dish. "I'll take the spoon and you can have the bowl."

I popped the brownies into the oven and set the timer that was sitting on the windowsill. Then I leaned back against the sink and started licking the wooden spoon while Greg worked on the bowl.

"Just tell me one thing," I pleaded. "What do you think is the secret of a good interview?"

"Well, I suppose you should have a few key questions, so that there aren't any humungus silences, but mainly you should just let it roll."

"You mean it'll have its own momentum."

"Exactly. Once that happens, you're home free."

"I hope you're right, Greg. It's my big chance."

"Your big chance for what?"

"Just my big chance," I said, regretting that I'd let that slip out.

Then I got very busy at the sink washing the utensils I had used.

"I'll never understand you," Greg muttered.

"Hand me the bowl," I said to Greg over my shoulder, "before you eat through the enamel."

"Here, he said, putting the bowl in the sink, "and just remember, this interview is not the end of the world. I mean, it's not like getting into college."

"I know," I said, vigorously scrubbing the egg beater. "It's a million times worse."

Greg sighed as he started walking out of the kitchen. "Like I said, I'll never understand you."

That's because you don't know what I'm talking about, I thought to myself. But he'd already disappeared, and I was spared having to make any explanations.

Now there wasn't much left for me to do except wait for the brownies to get done, get ready for bed, and hope.

CHAPTER 18 ——————

The next day I had a lot of trouble concentrating in class because all I could think about was the interview. It didn't help when I saw my friends at lunch. The first thing Gail did was advise me to make sure — no matter what — that I see him again.

"I know, I know," I agreed. "But how?"

"Maybe he'll ask you out," M.J. suggested.

"Forget it," I said.

"Maybe you could run out of pencils and have to continue the interview another time," Gail offered.

"Be serious," I begged.

"Just let things happen," Terry advised.

"But what if nothing does happen?" I asked.

Terry shrugged her shoulders, and for a moment I wished I could be as laid-back about life as she appeared to be.

When the bell rang and lunch period was

over, they all wished me good luck. Instead of making me feel better, that made me more nervous than ever. But I gritted my teeth, thanked them, and went off to class.

It wasn't easy for me to get through the next few periods without becoming totally unhinged. My last class was history, where Mr. Newell was going on about Jeffersonian democracy and how it relates to our government today. Ordinarily I would have been riveted, but I had trouble focusing on the subject and was relieved that he never got around to calling on me.

I dreaded, and at the same time couldn't wait for, the final bell. When it finally rang, I bolted out of the room and sped down the stairs to the music room, which is actually below the main floor. Besides being underground, it's soundproofed, which guarantees that no one can complain about the noise.

To my amazement, Len was already there, seated at the front of the room. He was actually sitting on the edge of the mini-stage, his guitar on his lap, looking very relaxed.

"Am I late?" I asked, rushing to the front of the room.

"How could you be? The bell just rang."

"Of course," I said, pulling a pad out of my canvas bag. "But it looks as though you've been waiting for me for hours."

"That's part of my act," he said, chuckling. "Take your time."

I fumbled frantically in my bag. "I don't know what happened to my pencils. I know

I had them in my history class." Then I remembered that I'd rushed out so fast I'd probably left them on my desk.

"Here, use this." Len handed me a ballpoint pen.

"Thanks," I said, taking the pen from him and feeling a certain electricity as my hand brushed his. I sat down in the front row.

Then, for the first time, I looked at him. I'd never seen him up close before. He was on the slim side, had longish straight brown hair, and although he really wasn't handsome, he had blue eyes that seemed to look straight through me. I couldn't stop looking at him.

"Aren't you going to ask me questions?" His smile was incredible.

"Sure," I said, giggling nervously. "That's why I'm here."

"I've made it easy for you," Len said, and pulled a crumbled piece of paper out of the back pocket of his jeans. "This will give you all the vital statistics — about when I first started playing guitar, about my mother being a music teacher and teaching me piano when I was six, about my father buying me a secondhand guitar when I was eight, which I wanted even more than a bike. All that boring stuff."

"This is great," I told him. "It'll really save time."

"I just did this in study hall, where I always do anything but study. I thought it would save you a lot of questions."

"It does." I glanced at the paper he'd

given me. "This takes care of all the basic information." I thought that he really had done me a big favor, but it also knocked out the key questions I had lined up.

I felt a moment of panic and then remembered what Greg had said about winging it. Well, here goes, I thought.

"Tell me something special," I said.

"Like what?" Len countered.

"Like . . . I don't know. Like how you feel when you play."

"Like I'm really into it. I guess you could say 'totally absorbed.' "

"You mean you don't think about anything else?"

"The music takes over."

"But how?"

"I can't answer that, but maybe I can let my fingers do the talking."

"Terrific," I said, thinking how lucky I was to have a private concert.

"What would you like to hear?" he asked, strumming a few chords.

For a moment my mind went completely blank. Then, out of nowhere, I said, " 'Greensleeves.' "

He tilted his head at me and smiled, saying, "That happens to be one of my favorites. I guess you're an old-fashioned girl."

"Guess so." I could feel myself blushing and bent my head over my pad and scribbled some notes in order to hide my self-consciousness.

My embarrassment didn't last long though, because as Len played the music, as he said, it took over. I actually forgot about myself. By the time he finished, I was completely enthralled, and I didn't say anything.

"Well?" he said, breaking the spell.

" 'Music like a curve of gold,' " I mumbled.

"Music like a curve of gold," Len repeated. "That's beautiful. Did you make it up?"

"It's from a poem by Sara Teasdale."

"How does it go?"

"I can't remember the whole poem, but I've never forgotten the lines: 'Life has loveliness to sell/ Music like a curve of gold/ Scent of pine trees in the rain/ Eyes that love you, arms that hold.' "

"Wow," Len said. "Gilman told me you were the *Swen*'s most literary writer. I guess he knew what he was talking about."

"I know more about poetry than I do about music," I confessed.

"We're like Jack Sprat and his wife. I don't know a thing about poetry."

"I could change all that," I said, surprised at my boldness.

"I wish you would," Len encouraged me. "My problem is I spend all my spare time playing guitar and listening to records and trying to compose."

"And I probably don't spend nearly enough time listening to music."

"I've got a great idea. A week from Saturday there's going to be a symposium on guitar music at the Y. It starts about one o'clock and goes on until late afternoon. How about coming with me?"

"I'd love to," I said, hardly able to contain my excitement.

"It might be a little heavy at times — everything from classical and jazz to the new stuff."

"I can't wait. I was excited thinking that now I would have some time to read up on the subject and practice playing.

"You're on! And now we better get back to the interview before they close up the school."

"You're right. Wouldn't it be terrible if we were locked up?" I lied.

"Just terrible," he agreed, smiling. "Problem is, I promised my folks I'd be home at six. It's my aunt's birthday and we're all going there for dinner. But now, back to the interview . . ."

"What would you like to talk about?" I asked, feeling considerably more secure now that I knew I was going to see him again.

"Ask me about punk rock," he answered.

"Tell me your feelings about punk," I obliged.

"Glad you asked," Len said. "Punk happens to be one of my pet hates."

"Why?"

"A lot of reasons. Most punk players are more interested in shocking and insulting their audiences than in making music. And they're usually terrible musicians."

"How did they get started?"

"They started as a protest against the commercialization of rock 'n' roll. Then they got carried away with their own awfulness — wearing safety pins as earrings and painting their hair purple."

Len went on and on about punk and switched to talking about Bruce Springsteen, who he believed represents all the positive aspects of rock. He said Springsteen plays with power and passion and deserves the adulation of the audience.

The rest of the interview was easy because Len enjoyed talking, and all I had to do was take notes, furiously, in order to keep up with him.

By the time the school guard came around, telling us we had to leave, I had plenty of information to write a good interview, but more important, I could look forward to going out with Len in less than twelve days.

We got ready to leave, Len putting his guitar in its case, and me carefully placing my pad of notes in my canvas bag. I was about to drop his ballpoint pen into my bag, too, when I remembered it didn't belong to me.

"Here," I said, ready to toss it to him. "I almost walked off with this."

"Keep it," Len insisted. "It'll serve as a reminder about a week from Saturday."

"Thanks," I said, as evenly as possible, knowing that my main problem between now and then would be to get my mind off that date.

CHAPTER 19 _____

I floated home in a daze, determined to play it cool, but the minute I saw Greg I spilled out the good news. He gave me the "I told you so" routine and went on about how I should take his advice more often. At that point he could have said anything, and it wouldn't have bothered me.

The next day at lunch, M.J. and Gail and Terry insisted that I give them a progress report, and they all congratulated me. Gail acted as though I'd won the 26-mile marathon, and she pointed out that if I could hang on to Len for less than five weeks from a week from Saturday, he was sure to ask me to the prom.

I had already figured that out, but I wanted everyone to get off my case so I asked Gail how she was doing.

"I'm still working on Tim," she admitted.

"I've decided that he's a little backward as far as women are concerned."

"Have you ever gotten him alone?" Terry asked.

"Not yet," Gail said, "but I'm working on it. I've managed to arrange for Tim and me to go, as a committee of two, to check out the refreshment possibilities. We're going to start making the rounds of some delis and sandwich suppliers this Saturday."

"And you're going to make that job last as long as possible," Terry commented.

"You're so right," Gail said, unabashedly. "It may take up to the afternoon of the last Saturday in May for us to make a decision."

Then M.J. turned to Terry and said, "Who have you decided to go with?"

"So far, I've only gotten a firm offer from Peter."

"Does that mean you're going with him?" I asked.

"Well," Terry replied, hesitating, "Peter's okay. He's sort of like an old shoe. Then there's Joey the Brain, and Golden Boy Dennis. They've both been dropping hints."

"What about Peter, then?" I wanted to know.

"I'm putting him on hold."

None of us bothered to ask how she planned to do that, but Terry has her ways and they always seem to work.

"Anyhow," Terry added, "I think we should talk about something else."

"Agreed," M.J. said, "and as long as you're willing to change the subject, I need your opinion. It's my parent's anniversary and I want to get them place mats and napkins. I can't decide between pink and white flowers or blue and white polka dots."

"I vote for the flowers," I said.

"Too feminine," Terry remarked. "Remember, it's an anniversary."

"What do you think, Gail?" M.J. asked.

"That's exactly the problem we're faced with on decorations for the prom. So far it hasn't been decided what color motif we should have. The girls on the committee want blue and the boys want red."

"You could compromise and have purple," I suggested.

"Good thinking," said Gail.

"You realize, of course, that we're back to that irresistible subject," Terry observed.

"It happens to be uppermost on our minds. Why fight it?" Gail shrugged her shoulders.

"It'd be a lot easier for me to talk about it if I knew I was even going," I muttered.

"You'll go," M.J. insisted. "Stop worrying."

"Well, if I don't get a date, I can always fake measles," I said with a sick laugh.

"Look, if worse comes to worse, Amy, you can go as a reporter for the *Swen*. Someone's got to write up the dance," Terry said.

"I'd rather die," I groaned. "Can you picture me wandering around, taking notes, while everyone else is having a good time?"

"You're right," Terry agreed. "I lost my head for a minute."

"I think I'll drown my troubles in a candy bar," I said, pushing my chair back. "Anybody want anything?"

"There's only one thing I want, and he's not for sale," Gail complained.

I giggled about that remark all the way to the candy machine, consoling myself that I wasn't the only one who was preoccupied with getting an invitation.

I had just plunked in my coins and pulled the lever for a Baby Ruth when I heard a familiar voice behind me.

"I've been looking for you. How'd it go and where is it?"

"Where's what?" I turned around slowly as though I didn't know it was Bob Gilman or what he was talking about.

"The interview, the interview," he repeated, as though I were a slow learner.

"Oh, hi, Bob," I said, wondering if by indirection he might learn some manners.

"Hi. Now tell me," he urged. "Did you get some good stuff and when can I see it?"

"Look," I answered, "the interview took place less than twenty-four hours ago. I'll write it up tonight and I'll get it to you tomorrow."

"Promise?"

"Promise."

"I'm not pressuring you or anything. It's just that we're on a tight schedule, and we can't be late for the printer."

"Of course," I said calmly, confident that I could deliver the goods.

"You're an ace!" Bob bellowed, backing away and in the process bumping into a small girl. "Careful, kid," he mumbled to her. Then, pointing his finger at me, he said dictatorially, "See you in the *Swen* office tomorrow A.M. as soon as the first bell rings. Deal?"

"Deal," I said agreeably. I knew that the reason I could remain so polite, even though Bob was so rude, was that I was just as anxious as he was to get the interview out of the way. Then I could settle down to some serious studying about the guitar and rock and "all that jazz."

CHAPTER 20 ⸻

That night I polished off the interview. I started with Len saying he let his fingers do the talking and went on from there. Everything fell into place, and I delivered the interview to Bob at the *Swen* office before classes the next day.

"Glad you're on time," Bob said, as I handed him the interview. He was seated behind a desk at the front of the room. "Now sit down while I read it, in case I want revisions."

"Okay," I said, even though it made me very uncomfortable to watch someone read what I'd written. What if he hated it!

It seemed to take him an agonizingly long time, but it was actually less than seven minutes because he finished before the second bell rang (the bells are spaced seven minutes apart). I waited nervously for his verdict, and before he said anything, he nodded his head several times.

"Not bad," he deigned to say. "We'll roll it."

"You mean you like it the way it is?" I couldn't believe he didn't find something to change.

"I said we'd roll it, didn't I?" He sounded like his usual impatient self, but there was a twinkle in his eye and I knew he was pleased.

I hurried to my first class, relieved that I'd successfully passed that hurdle and could spend all my free time preparing for Len. It was lucky I had always gotten good grades, because I hoped to get by on my reputation and do a minimum of work the next ten days.

That day after school I rushed home. It was lucky that neither Kenny or Greg were around so I didn't have to explain why I hadn't followed my usual routine of going to the library.

After fortifying myself with a brownie and a glass of milk, I went to my room. The first book I attacked was on rock stars. I figured if I had a few bits of inside information about five or six biggies, I could hold Len's attention.

I listed a few interesting items such as the fact that Eddie Money had been a cop in New York City before becoming a rock star with two L.P.'s that sold more than three million; or that Meat Loaf, who looks more jolly than sexy because of his ample physique, cut an album called *Bat out of Hell* that went double platinum — almost three million copies sold. Before his phenomenal success, he was a theatrical performer for Joseph Papp, the New York Public Theater director.

In order to keep my brains from getting scrambled with too much information, I decided to practice the guitar. If I got into a situation where I could actually play a few pieces, Lenny would be amazed.

I kept up that routine for the next ten days. I tried to get most of my homework done in study hall, but a couple of afternoons I did go to the library, just to get my math out of the way. One of those times I was hurriedly trying to get through my assignment when Jeff passed by, carrying a load of books. He backed up, stopped by my table, and said over his shoulder, "Haven't seen you lately. Don't you like working here anymore?"

"Oh, sure," I answered quickly. "It's just that I've got a lot of things to do at home this week."

"Well, maybe when you have time, I'll fill you in on some of the advance copies we've received."

"I'd like that," I said. "Like right now."

He put the stack of books on the table and leaned against it. He lowered his voice and gave me a brief rundown on the latest Philip Roth book.

I could feel my heart beat faster, just listening to Jeff. No one else had that effect on me. But why couldn't we talk about anything personal?

Just then, Ms. Kruger passed by and shot us a look that was a combination frown and smile. She didn't say anything, but Jeff got the message, picked up the stack of books that had been on the table, and mouthed the word "Later."

I went back to my math, still feeling a glow from Jeff's being so close to me. However, I knew his interest in me was purely academic. The wise thing for me to do was hurry up with my homework and go home so I could spend some time on my guitar project.

I guess I was fooling myself if I thought I could keep my family from asking questions about my sudden interest in guitar. They weren't aware that I was reading up on the subject so extensively, but they couldn't help hearing me practice. And my mother, who notices everything, remarked one night at dinner that I must really be fascinated by the instrument because she didn't think anything could get me to cut my fingernails.

"Only on my left hand," I told her.

"Now we know what to get you for your birthday," my father said. "Sixteen is an important one."

"That's a great idea!" I shouted. "This old thing of Greg's is falling apart."

"But Amy wanted a typewriter," my mother said. "Isn't that right, Aim?"

"I think maybe a guitar is a better idea. In

fact, since my birthday isn't for a couple of months, maybe I could get my present early."

"We'll think about it," my mother said cautiously.

The truth was, I had desperately wanted an electric typewriter I could take to college. But the guitar would be such a good conversation piece; I mean, it would open up all kinds of discussion with Len. I could ask his opinion about the various types, what kind I should get — maybe even get him to go looking around for one with me.

For a minute I had this fantasy of Len and me, hand in hand, ambling into music stores, researching the different instruments.

"Amy, come back to this planet," Greg teased me. "You look like you're on Mars."

"Just thinking about something," I answered vaguely. I must have really been out to lunch because my parents had already left the table and Kenny and Greg had started cleaning up.

I got up to help and went to the sink with my hands filled with dishes. I started to rinse them under hot water before putting them in the dishwasher.

"Ouch," I screeched as the water poured over my hands. I dropped the plate I was holding and it shattered into a million pieces.

"What happened?" Kenny yelped. "You sound like you're on fire."

"You can see what happened," I said sharply. "Haven't you ever broken a dish in your life?"

"Sure," Kenny replied seriously. "Plenty of times. But you never do."

I gingerly blotted my left hand with a paper towel, trying to keep back the tears. Greg was watching me intently, then grasped my left hand by the wrist and stared in amazement at my fingertips.

"These look awful," he said. "They must be killing you."

My fingertips were all swollen and puffy, and there were dents on the tips. They had actually bled a little the previous night, but I would never admit that.

"They're okay," I murmured. I'd read somewhere that guitar players had to develop callouses. "I'm just trying to toughen up."

"But not overnight, dummy. It takes weeks, and it should be gradual." I knew he was genuinely concerned, but he just made me upset.

"Leave me alone, will you?"

Kenny came running over to see what was going on. He took one look at my sore fingers and said, "Yuck."

That was all I needed to really set me off. "Leave me alone, both of you," I snapped. Then I tore out of the kitchen, upstairs to my room, slammed the door, and burst into tears.

I wasn't sure if I was crying because my fingers still hurt, because I knew I'd never learn the guitar in time to show Len on Saturday, or because it was getting closer to Junior Prom time and I still had no idea if I was going. Probably all three. I also knew

I had to pull myself together. That meant taking a hot bath — being careful to keep my left hand out of the water — and then attacking a chapter entitled "The Political Significance of Guitar Music." One thing I learned a long time ago is that it doesn't do any good to mope.

CHAPTER 21 ——————

L en and I arranged to meet at the Y promptly at twelve forty-five to make sure we'd get decent seats. I actually arrived a few minutes before him and waited inside the foyer in order to avoid the cold. I was leaning against the wall, watching the people who were already crowding into the auditorium, when Len approached. His blue eyes were sparkling brighter than ever.

"You're a woman of your word," he said, squeezing my shoulder.

"You told me to be on time," I remarked, not letting on that I'd been ready to leave my house since about nine o'clock that morning.

"This place has been sold out for days, and I knew if we didn't get here early it might be standing-room-only." He grabbed my hand and pulled me toward the auditorium. Then he handed the tickets to the usher and led the way to a couple of seats in one of the last rows.

"Why so far back?" I asked. "There are still plenty of seats."

"Because if it gets boring, we can split and not be too obvious."

I looked at the program the usher had handed us. "I'm sure it'll be fascinating. I see that Mel Bernstein, who's head of new talent for a record company, is one of the key speakers. He's going to talk about possible ways to get into the field."

"Could be a drag," Len said, to my amazement.

As a matter of fact, Len was right — a lot of the program was a drag. But I wouldn't say so for fear that the parts I didn't like might be the same parts that Len did like. After all, he was the expert. Also, it gave me an opportunity to show how much I knew.

For example, when some speaker was going on about classical guitar and how the group, Pink Floyd, incorporated classical training into their rock music, I muttered something about their "spacy lyrical motifs" and that "The Dark Side of the Moon" made in 1973 was one of the most successful albums of the decade.

I waited for Len to respond but he just looked at me and didn't say anything.

And when some critic was talking about The Who and Pete Townshend, their lead guitarist and one of the greatest in the world,

I leaned over to Len and whispered, "The first rock opera, *Tommy*, was written by Townshend in 1968."

"Oh really," Len said, as though he couldn't care less.

During the intermission we bumped into Chuck Gill and Fran Norton. They are both juniors and good friends of Len's. Chuck, who is on the chunky side and very jovial, invited us to go back to his house as soon as the program was over.

"My folks are home playing bridge, but they said we could use the kitchen and the rec room. Fran is going to make her specialty, lasagna."

"Lasagna is the only thing I can make," Fran said, smiling. "But I have a foolproof recipe." Fran had a very friendly manner that perfectly matched her looks — curly blond hair, green eyes, and dimples. I liked her right away.

"How about it?" Len asked me.

"I love lasagna," I told him.

"You're on!" Chuck said. "We'll meet you in the lobby as soon as this is over and make tracks for my house. I live only six blocks away."

After the intermission I tried hard to show how interested I was in what was going on — even when some musicologist droned on about the difference between hard rock, which is "heavy and angular," and surf rock, which he described as "Anglo-Saxon music, relying on melody."

Actually, I was relieved when it was over, but of course I'd never admit it. When we met Chuck and Fran and started walking toward Chuck's house, Len asked me how I likèd the program.

"Great," I enthused, lying.

"Really?" Len commented. "I thought most of it was pretty boring."

"Well, some of it was," I said, hedging. "I mean, who doesn't know that rock is based on basic blues chord progressions?"

"Everybody, obviously, even you." I couldn't tell if Len was making fun of me or not, but I let it pass.

When we got to Chuck's house, we dumped our parkas on the hall bench, waved briefly to his folks who were in the living room concentrating on their game. Chuck told us in a stage whisper that there's an unwritten rule that bridge players are not to be spoken to while playing, upon penalty of death. Of course, that made everyone laugh — even the bridge players — and then we rapidly disappeared into the kitchen where the ingredients for the lasagna were lined up.

"You didn't forget a thing, not even the Parmesan cheese," Fran exclaimed.

"That would be like playing with fewer than five strings," I said. Nobody reacted to what I said; maybe they didn't understand the comparison.

After Fran prepared everything and shoved it in the oven to bake, Chuck suggested we go downstairs to the rec room and play some records until it was time to eat. "I've got some new disco albums," he told us.

"Disco," I said in a surprised voice.

"What's wrong with disco?" Chuck asked, as he led the way downstairs to the rec room.

"Yeah, what's wrong with disco?" Fran chimed in.

I noticed Len didn't say anything, but I was sure he wouldn't think too highly of it. Therefore, I thought I was on safe ground when I said, "It's awfully repetitive."

"So what?" said Len. "It still has lyrical content and is good to dance to."

"Guess so," I mumbled.

Chuck put on a record and we did dance, although "mess around" would be a more accurate description. We keep changing partners and at one point Fran was dancing with me and Chuck and Len were partners. The whole scene struck us as being hilarious, and for a while I was having so much fun that I actually forgot my purpose. When Chuck put on a recording by the Human Switchboard, I said, "That's one of those new wave groups that is a reaction to the conventionalism that rock has become up to this time."

Len simply frowned, and when I thought about it later — much later — when I morbidly reviewed my whole relationship with Len, I realized that *he* was trying to reach *me* on my level.

When we'd gone back upstairs, Chuck and Fran were involved in making a salad and

Len and I were sitting at the round butcher block table at the other end of the kitchen.

"I found that poem," Len said, out of the blue.

"What poem?" I asked. I didn't know what he was talking about.

"The one that goes; 'Spend all you have for loveliness. Buy it and never count the cost; For one white singing hour of peace, Count many a year of strife well lost.'"

"Oh, that's called 'Barter,'" I said.

"I know," said Len. "I looked it up in our anthology at home. I even memorized it."

"You did?" I was rather amazed.

"It really made me think — especially the last line that goes: 'And for a breath of ecstasy, Give all you have been, or could be.'" He looked very thoughtful and then asked, "Do you believe in that — sacrificing everything for a 'breath of ecstasy'?"

I did have a number of ideas, but I was reluctant to share them. I mean I didn't want him to think I was hung up on poetry so I tried to get back on his track.

"It's lucky if you can combine what you love doing — in your case playing the guitar — and making it practical at the same time. That would make it 'practically ecstatic.'"

"I like that idea," he said, but he seemed to want to get off the subject of himself. "What about what you like to do? Don't you feel terrific when you write something and you know it's good?"

"Sure," I admitted, "but there must be nothing like making beautiful music."

His blue eyes narrowed as he looked through me. He must have known I was exaggerating, because then he said. "There are other things in the world."

"I suppose so, but I think guitar playing is the greatest."

"Right now, the only practically ecstatic thing for me would be some food." Then he shouted to Fran and Chuck, "Hey you guys, I'm starving."

Just then the timer went off, and Chuck quipped, "The master has spoken," and Fran added, "The lasagna is ready," and Len turned to me and said, "You didn't know I had magical powers, did you.?"

"I'm not surprised," I said flatteringly. Meanwhile I was thinking why couldn't some of that magic rub off on us.

CHAPTER 22 _____

The rest of the evening was uneventful, but in retrospect it wasn't much fun, either. It seemed to me that Len left me out of the conversation. I thought perhaps that was because Chuck and Fran and Len were all juniors and shared a lot of the same classes. Still, I thought Len could have made some effort to include me.

At one point Fran asked me if I'd written any short stories, or if I was only interested in doing articles and interviews.

"I've done a few short stories for my English class, and Ms. Newman has given me a lot of encouragement. She says I should submit them to the literary magazine, but I don't think they're good enough."

"No harm in trying," Fran said. "The worst that can happen is you'll be turned down." Then she added wistfully, "I always wanted to be a writer."

119

"According to Amy, the only important thing in the world is being a guitar player," Len cracked.

At that moment I knew I'd overplayed my enthusiasm for the guitar. I also felt put down, and for the rest of the evening I didn't say much.

After we'd finished eating and were cleaning up, Chuck announced that he hated to be a party pooper but that he was in training for the swim team, which meant getting to bed before eleven.

"I've already warned Fran that I turn into a pumpkin then," he said, turning to Len who was drying the lasagna dish, "but I forgot to tell you and Amy."

"That's okay," Len said, a little too quickly, I thought. "It's been a long day and I want to get up early and do some practicing."

"By the way," Fran asked, "are you going to be playing at the Junior Prom?"

I could feel my heart beat faster when I heard the words "junior prom." It was a subject I'd studiously avoided all night, but I was hoping someone else would bring it up.

"Playing at dances is not my scene," Len said, "but I was flattered that the entertainment committee asked me. I think they're using the Glad Hands. They're really the best in the school for dance music."

"But you're going to the prom," I murmured, half to myself. It just slipped out and then I almost died of embarrassment.

"Who isn't?" Len remarked, ending the discussion.

I would have happily disappeared then. There was nothing I could say so I made a big thing of wiping off the butcher block table with a sponge. I acted as though my life depended on getting it scrubbed to perfection.

Then I was saved, because Fran announced that we better get going.

"We don't want to be responsible for corrupting our swim star," Fran said.

"I'll drive you all home," Chuck volunteered. "My father told me earlier it was okay for me to use the car, as long as I didn't break training."

"You mean you're susceptible to a bribe," Len said, laughing. He looked so cute and had such a good sense of humor that I felt worse than ever when I faced the fact that I'd probably never go out with him again.

"It's not really a bribe," Chuck explained, "because my father knows I believe in making sacrifices for the swim team. It's more like a reward."

"Whatever it is, we're all benefiting," Fran said. "Let's get moving."

We went into the hall to get our things and whispered good-bye to the bridge players. Chuck's mother looked up long enough to say, "Drive carefully," which seems to be an automatic response for all mothers, and we were off.

Len and I piled into the back seat of the

Honda, and I sat as close to him as our parkas would permit. But he didn't seem interested enough in me to even hold my hand.

"First stop will be Amy," Chuck announced.

"That makes sense," Len said.

Actually, it didn't matter who was dropped off first, because we all lived within walking distance of school. The fact that Chuck wanted to drop me first and Len agreed so quickly made me feel as though they were both anxious to unload me.

When we arrived at my house, Len said, "I'll walk you to your door."

That's the least he can do, I thought to myself. By that time I was so paranoid I took everything the wrong way.

I said good-bye to Fran and Chuck and thanked them for dinner. Then I headed for our front door, fumbling in my parka pocket for my key. Len was standing next to me as I opened the door, and I was hoping against hope that he'd say something encouraging, something that would show he wanted to see me again.

"Well," I said hesitantly.

"Well," he echoed.

"I hope I see you again," I blurted out, amazed at my own boldness.

"Bound to happen," he said. "We do go to the same school."

I would have thought that was a really mean remark, but he was smiling so I knew he was half-kidding.

"Thanks for today," I said, trying to sound a lot lighter than I felt.

"You're welcome," Len said evenly. Then he leaned over and kissed me on the cheek. It wasn't exactly romantic, but for a minute I was hopeful that all was not lost. Then my hopes were completely shattered when he back away, turned toward the car, waved his hand at me over his shoulder, and said, "Have a nice life!"

CHAPTER 23 _____

Have a nice life, I kept repeating to myself as I stood under the shower which I'd turned on full blast, wishing it would pound away all my problems. I must have stood there twenty minutes, and when I finally emerged my skin was tingling, but I didn't feel any better.

It was too late to call M.J. and confide in her, but at least I had that to look forward to the next morning. That was about all I had to look forward to. I certainly wasn't overjoyed at the prospect of answering a lot of questions from my family about my date with Len.

To make myself feel better, I kept trying to come up with some reasons why he wasn't all that great. It wasn't easy. The worst thing about him was that he wasn't interested in me.

It must have taken me hours to fall asleep, because when I woke up it was after eleven o'clock. I splashed some cold water on my face, and dragged myself downstairs, still wearing my pajamas and my old red plaid robe. My mother was alone in the kitchen, preparing a turkey, which she often does on the weekend.

"Hi sweetie," she said as I shuffled into the kitchen. "How'd it go?"

"Okay," I replied. I guess my lack of enthusiasm was obvious and she didn't ask any questions. I felt I should say something, without going into the gory details, so I added, "I've changed my mind about wanting a guitar for my birthday. I'll stick with my electric typewriter idea."

"Good thinking!" my mother approved, and she smiled knowingly.

I couldn't help smiling, too, and for the first time since the previous evening I was beginning to feel human.

"Where is everyone?" I asked.

"Dad has gone to play tennis, Kenny is bike-riding with Scott, and Greg went to the store for me. Can you believe I forgot to buy stuffing for the turkey?"

"I can believe anything," I muttered.

My mother glanced at me and was about to say something when Greg charged in the back door.

"Here are the goods," he said, handing the bundle he was holding to my mother. Then he looked at me. "You look like something the cat *wouldn't* drag in."

"Thanks," I said dryly.

"Well, you must have had a heavy evening. Your eyes are half-closed and you aren't even dressed yet."

"You're very observant," I commented.

"How was superstar?" he asked.

"He's okay."

"But . . ." Greg sounded curious.

"But nothing."

"But you're not going to see him again."

"Why don't you have some breakfast?" my mother interrupted. "I'll make you some eggs if you want, Amy."

"No thanks. I'll settle for Grapenuts." I took the box out of the cupboard and opened the fridge for some milk.

"I'm going over to David's house for a jam session. We're trying out a new wrinkle — Polly Martin is going to sing with us. She's a young edition of Bette Midler," Greg told us.

"I hear the Glad Hands are doing the prom," I said. I guess I was trying to get back at him for being so gross about my success — or lack of it — with Len.

"You can't win 'em all," Greg murmured, shrugging his shoulders.

"So I've noticed," I said significantly.

I wondered if Greg really felt so indifferent or was just putting up a good front. I wished I could be more like Greg when it came to faking it, but I can't seem to hide my feelings no matter how hard I try.

As soon as I finished my Grapenuts I went upstairs and called M.J. I spilled everything out, and M.J. listened without saying anything until I was finished bemoaning my fate.

"A million things can happen between now and the last Saturday in May," she said.

"But I've had two perfect opportunities and I didn't get to first base with either of them."

"And they didn't get to first base, either," M.J. chuckled. "Think of it that way."

"That's not because I wouldn't let them," I said, laughing in spite of myself.

"Well, just try not to dwell on the past," M.J. advised.

"Then I'll think about the future, and that means thinking about the prom," I wailed.

"You shouldn't do that either," M.J. said.

"That's like telling someone to stand in a corner and not think about a white bear. It's impossible to do."

"Why don't you try concentrating on the present? I mean, just live from day to day and see what happens."

"And what if nothing happens?" I asked.

"I guarantee you something will. It always has, hasn't it?"

"You're right about that, I guess."

"Now about today. They're showing *2001* on Home Box Office. How about coming over and watching? I'll ask Gail and Terry, too."

"I'd love it." I suddenly felt a lot better about life. "And I'll bring enough popcorn for all of us."

"Terrific," M.J. said. "The movie starts at two-thirty so I'll see you then."

"Later," I said, and hung up, thinking that no one would ever need a psychiatrist if they had a friend like M.J.

CHAPTER 24 _____

I tried to do what M.J. suggested — that is,
concentrate on the present. It wasn't
easy and I wasn't too successful.

That Monday I returned all my music books
to the library and was relieved that Jeff
wasn't there to make some remark that might
put me on the spot. I decided to get back into
my routine of going to the library every day
to do my homework.

On Tuesday I felt an unexpected pang
when again I noticed Jeff wasn't anywhere to
be seen in the library. I made a circuitous
route to the back of the room where I usually
sit, but he wasn't there. I had completed my
assignments and was heading for the door
when I noticed that Sally Finch was at the
checkout desk. Sally was a copy editor on
the *Swen* and I'd seen her in the newspaper
office. She was a senior and about five feet

ten. Her shoulders were always hunched over, as though that would make her shrink.

She was never very friendly but I knew she was painfully shy. And even when someone spoke to her, her eyes darted around as though she were looking for an escape hatch. I also knew she would only speak to someone when spoken to.

I was surprised at how anxious I was to find out about Jeff — I mean, we'd never actually had a relationship, but I suddenly missed him. I missed not reading any good books for a long time, too, and now I wanted to find out what had come in that he might recommend. Or was I really yearning for Jeff? I wouldn't allow myself to think of him in those terms.

Sally was sitting on the stool behind the checkout desk, her head buried in a book. I had a feeling she was hiding more than she was reading. But like everyone, I know what it is to be shy, and I thought she might actually appreciate my talking to her.

"Hi, Sally," I said. "Haven't seen you here before."

"Hi," she answered.

"Have you been here long?"

"No."

She certainly wasn't making it easy for me to talk to her, so I thought I might as well get to the point.

"What happened to Jeff?" I asked.

"Sick," she replied.

"Sick!" I repeated in an alarmed voice. "What is it?"

"Flu," she said.

"There's a lot of it around," I said, relieved that he didn't have anything more serious. "Will he be out long?"

"A week or two." Sally seemed anxious to get back to her book, and I could take a hint.

"See ya," I said, and headed for the door.

All the way home I debated with myself whether I should send a get-well card to Jeff. Ordinarily, it wouldn't be a big deal — I mean, I'd just send one and forget about it. But Jeff was different, special I guess, as far as I was concerned, and he might take it the wrong way. Actually, I didn't know if he was even interested in girls. I'd seen him at a number of school events, but he was always with a group of kids and never seemed to be part of a couple. Sort of like me, come to think of it.

Anyhow, I decided it would be stupid to pay attention to him now just because he was sick. Especially since the last couple of times he'd tried to get me involved in a conversation I'd practically snubbed him. That was because I'd been preoccupied with my basketball and guitar projects.

CHAPTER 25 ─────────────

It was almost the end of April and my prospects of being invited to the prom seemed dimmer than ever.

I tried to keep my sense of humor and at one time suggested to M.J. that if I was lucky I might break a leg — even two legs — and that would be an excellent excuse for not going to a dance. M.J. said that on top of that maybe I could get a really bad strep throat, and then I wouldn't be able to answer questions about whom I had been planning to go with.

We went on like that, dreaming up more and more dire reasons why I would have to stay home on that crucial night. But as it got closer to JP Day, my sense of humor started to fade.

Then one Friday I was sitting at Rico's with M.J. and Terry, wondering when Gail would appear. We had just ordered our Cokes when she blew in, more excited than usual. Even before she sat down, she exclaimed breathlessly, "He asked me! He asked me!"

No one had to ask what she was talking about. We all knew that she meant Tim Durwood had invited her to the prom.

"Nice work," Terry said, and M.J. said, "Congratulations," and I said, "How'd ya do it?"

To be honest, I felt torn. On the one hand, I really was glad Gail's problems were over. Even though she comes on a little strong sometimes, I like her a lot, and she is the kind of girl who will go out of her way for a friend. On the other hand, I felt deserted. Now I was the only one of the four of us who didn't have a date for the prom. I felt like Orphan Annie without Sandy; or even worse, I felt like Sandy without his "Arf."

Gail was going on about how it had all come about. "It was totally unexpected when he finally got around to asking me. Actually, he didn't *ask* me, he *told* me."

"What do you mean?" Terry asked.

"We were having this big debate in the committee about what time the prom should begin — seven-thirty or eight o'clock. I said we should compromise and have it start at a quarter to eight. Everyone except Tim, who seemed bored with the whole subject, kicked that idea around for a while, but we couldn't come to a decision."

"And then?" M.J. asked.

"And then it was time to leave. Everyone

left in a hurry, except Tim and me. He seemed to want to talk, but he didn't say anything so naturally I tried to help him out."

"I wish I could learn your technique," I sighed.

"It was easy. I just continued talking about what was the best time for the prom to begin and asked him what he thought since he hadn't said anything at the meeting. He took the longest time to answer, and then he said, 'Quarter to eight, of course.' I asked him why, and he said in a rather offhand, sophisticated manner, 'Because that's when my date wants it to begin.'"

"And you said . . ." M.J. asked.

"I made some retarded remark about 'Your date, who's your date?' and he said, in the most melting tones you can imagine, 'You are, Gail, if you want to be.' I almost fainted dead away, but I managed to pull myself together enough to say, 'Timmy, I'd love to.'"

"That the most romantic invitation I ever heard," Terry said, obviously impressed.

"Who have you decided to go with?" Gail asked Terry. We all knew that Terry was debating whether to go with Joey, the junior class intellectual who also happened to be good-looking and had had a crush on Terry for centuries, or with Dennis, who was president of the junior class and number two on the tennis team.

"You'll never believe this," Terry said, "but I'm going with Eric."

"Eric!" we all shouted at once. "When did that happen?"

"It just happened. Yesterday, to be exact."

"What about Joey and Dennis? I thought they were the only ones in the running," Gail said.

"They were, but both Joey and Dennis took it for granted I was going with them. Joey, who is probably going to get early admission to Harvard, is a wimp when it comes to women. And Dennis is so conceited he couldn't believe that anyone would turn down his invitation."

"How did you even get to know Eric?" I asked.

"It was very natural. He was taking pictures of the gymnastics team for the yearbook, and afterwards he asked me if I'd show him some special tricks on the balance beam. Since gymnastics is my favorite thing in life — besides boys — I agreed. He really appreciated the time I took to explain all the moves to him. Then afterwards we got into this long discussion about how he knew he would always take pictures, if not professionally, then as a hobby, and I told him I hoped I could do gymnastics until I got old and gray. We seemed to agree on a lot of things."

"But how'd he happen to ask you to the prom?" I wanted to know.

"He mentioned that he was going to be one of several photographers to take pictures at the prom, and would I like to go with him even though he couldn't stick with me the whole time."

"And you said yes," M.J. said.

"I said yes," Terry said, "because if there's one thing I don't like it's being glued at the hip to whoever takes me to a dance. Joey would never let me out of his sight, and Dennis is so conceited he'd probably get into a fistfight if I danced with anyone else. Eric seems as though he'll be just right for me."

"You're so lucky," I groaned.

"Stop worrying. You've still got three weeks," Terry said.

"And I didn't find out until today that I was going for sure," Gail added.

"I suppose," I mumbled, but I was less and less convinced that anything good would happen to me between now and the last Saturday in May.

After we left Rico's that afternoon, M.J. and I were walking home and I made a feeble attempt at humor.

"What do you think is the best way to break a leg?" I asked.

But at that point, M.J. was feeling so much empathy for me that even she couldn't bring herself to laugh.

"We'll think of something," she said. "A lot can happen in three weeks."

CHAPTER 26 ———————

The last place in the world I expected to meet someone who might be interested in me romantically was in the science lab. Personally, I can't imagine a more antiseptic, unromantic place. Besides having a distinct odor of formaldehyde, the atmosphere is sterile. I have a feeling that a fresh-cut flower would drop dead in there.

The strange thing about our school is that it's supposed to be an honor and privilege to work in the science lab where we can dissect frogs and fetal pigs. Yuck! In fact, it's only in the last half of the year that tenth-graders are allowed to invade the premises. Then, because we're so inexperienced in the mysteries of dissection, we are linked up with more advanced students.

Mr. Kravitz, our teacher, explained that we had to draw numbers for partners. "There are twelve tenth-graders and twelve eleventh-graders, and as far as I'm concerned, the selection is random, undetermined by human input, and in the laps of the gods."

This was a typical Kravitz statement, and one reason why I had so much trouble with his course. He talked in circles. Fortunately, I could understand the textbook, but I was totally at a loss after one of his lectures.

There was a number on each of the twelve lab tables, and after we picked our slips, we went to the table designated. I was lucky, I suppose, because my Brother Rat, which is what we call our partners, was Hank Boas. I'd never met him before, but I knew he was one of the brains of the junior class. He had a reputation for being brilliant, never got less than an A in any subject, and was head of the science club.

Hank was tall, lanky, beak-nosed, and a little like the absentminded professor, even though he was only seventeen. But I liked him right away because he was totally guileless. Obviously he wasn't interested in clothes. They hung on him as if they were on a hanger, and the color combinations were not to be believed — an orange plaid shirt under a bright red sweater.

The first thing Hank said to me, after we introduced ourselves, was, "You're cute. I was hoping I'd get you for a partner." He said it matter-of-factly, as though he were commenting on the weather.

"Thank you," I said, slightly flabbergasted.

"I think I'm lucky to get you. I mean, you do have a reputation in the science department."

"That's because nobody else cares as much as I do. I already know I want to be a scientist. Both my parents are doctors."

"You're lucky," I said. "Not everyone can be so sure about what they want to do while they're still in high school."

"I was born knowing." He said it in such a way that he wasn't at all obnoxious. I had to admire his confidence, even though he was a bit odd.

"All right, people," Mr. Kravitz said in an official tone, "frog time."

Then he proceeded to walk around the room, placing a dead frog in a plastic bag on each table. He talked all the time, explaining that frogs are vertebrates and enough like ourselves to throw some light on our own structure and function.

"Never thought I resembled a frog," I whispered to Hank.

"You're much prettier," he said, deadly serious. It bothered me a little that he wasn't being funny.

"Attention, people," Kravitz was saying. "Step one: Remove frog from the plastic bag and pin it to the dissecting pan. For you first-timers, your partner will show you how it's done."

Hank deftly pinned the frog down and I muttered, "I'll never eat frogs legs again."

"You *are* cute," Hank said, looking at me as though I was an unique specimen.

I didn't know quite how to handle him. He'd already called me cute twice, and once implied I was pretty. It flashed through my mind that neither Grant or Len had gotten around to complimenting me on my looks. Maybe Hank was a new possibility.

The rest of the period Kravitz kept up a running commentary on how to use the scissors and scalpel to cut through the ventral wall and the procedure for separating the skin from the body. Then he drew a picture of the insides of a frog on the blackboard and labeled the various organs. He told us to locate the heart, liver, gall bladder, stomach, and on and on.

I couldn't tell the difference between the liver and the kidney. When I pointed out to Hank that they were both reddish-brown, he said I had a good eye — but not for science.

Just before class was over, Kravitz announced that we should write a report on everything we'd investigated, relate it to the human body, and state its purpose.

"Oh, no," I mumbled. "I don't know the pancreas from the pyloric valve."

Hank laughed out loud. "You're wonderful!" he exclaimed. "A complete innocent! How about meeting me in Study Hall 303 after school? It's usually empty, and I can help you with the report."

"Would you? That would be terrific."

"It'll be my pleasure. I happen to be a very good teacher but I don't get much opportunity to use my teaching talent."

"I'll be there as soon as school's over, and you can practice on me."

"There's nothing I'd like better, Amy." Then I was sure he mumbled something about finding a frog's heart and losing his own, but he seemed to be talking to himself and I wasn't sure I should be listening.

Then he said in a clear voice, "I'll clean up the debris and you can wash off the scissors and scalpel. Okay?"

"Okay," I said, relieved that I didn't have to cope with the remains of the frog.

As I waited in line at the sink, I couldn't help thinking that Hank was a junior, and as far as I knew unattached. I would have to overlook the fact that he was slightly off the wall. He was my last chance.

CHAPTER 27 ⸻

Hank was already in 303 when I arrived, hunched over a desk and so deeply engrossed in doing something that he didn't see me when I came in. I cleared my throat three times, but still he didn't look up. Then I knocked loudly on the desk where he was sitting and he finally noticed me.

"Oh, you're here," he remarked. "I'll be right with you."

He went back to whatever he was doing, while I dumped my things on an empty desk and then sat down next to him.

"There," he said, "now this will make everything crystal clear."

He showed me a sketch of a frog's and a human's insides. Lines were drawn between their corresponding parts, and it made it very easy to make a comparison between the two.

"You've made it so simple. I never could

142

have figured that out by myself." I meant it, too, although it may have sounded like sheer flattery.

"Now all you have to do is write the purpose of every organ. Easy."

"Easy," I agreed, "if you happen to know the purpose."

Hank shook his head, as though I were a hopeless case, but he was smiling. "Take some notes, and I'll explain everything. Then all you have to do is write everything up. Zap, and you'll have a report."

He described all the parts of the body and their functions, while I jotted down notes. He was amazingly clear and easy to follow. When he was finished, I told him that he really was a good teacher. "I know," he remarked. "I find this stuff fascinating."

"I would too if I knew more." I was back to being agreeable. "Do you do any experiments at home?"

"I happen to be a gerbil freak. At last count I had seven."

"Seven!" I repeated, astonished.

"They reproduce like crazy. Maybe you'd like to see my collection."

"Sure," I said, thinking that this would give me an opportunity to see him again.

"How about right now? I live on Mulberry Street. Where do you live?"

"On Ash."

"That's perfect. You can stop by and if you like the idea, I could help you start your own gerbil community."

"Terrific," I lied. As far as I was concerned it would be like setting up a condominium for rats.

"Come on then." He grabbed his jacket and headed for the door. I picked up my things and trailed behind, reluctant to manufacture an excuse for not going with him, and reluctant to seem uninterested in his project. My need to please won out and I hurried to catch up to him.

All the way to his house he babbled on about gerbils — how inquisitive and friendly they are; how their tails are their most important asset, acting as a stabilizer; how they can jump eighteen inches horizontally. Since there was very little I could say on the subject, I asked a lot of questions. Hank seemed to be delighted to answer them even though I thought I came across as a dummy.

We went in the back door of his house where a young French woman was peeling potatoes over the sink.

"Hello, Henri," she greeted him.

"Hello, Françoise. This is my friend, Amy."

"Hello, Amy." Françoise extended her hand to me and I shook it.

"Amy is here to see my gerbils. Maybe she'll start a commune of her own."

"Oh no," Françoise wailed. "Already there are too much gerbils in the world."

"Too many," Hank corrected her. "Although actually not enough."

"Too many," Françoise repeated, and went back to peeling.

"Follow me," Hank instructed, and he led me down the back stairs to the cellar, which was surprisingly well lit and dry.

"Who's Françoise?" I couldn't help asking. She was dressed in a sweater and skirt and looked more like a college girl than a housekeeper.

"She's a French student living with us in order to learn English. In exchange for room and board, she helps out with the housework. She'll be going back to France this summer."

"She seems nice," I remarked.

"She is. Her only problem is she's turned off by gerbils."

"Oh, really." I realized then that I'd better change my attitude, or Hank might be turned off by me.

It wasn't going to be easy, but I tried to keep an open mind as I stood beside the cage that housed Hank's gerbils. The cage was quite large, made of plastic, and its floor was covered with sawdust. There was one gerbil, obviously the mother, who was much bigger than her six babies. I had to admit they were kind of cute, but I wasn't that anxious to hold them.

Hank took one of the babies out of the cage, explaining that the proper way to hold it was to support its weight on one hand and hold it at the base of the tail with the other hand.

"You should never grasp a gerbil by the tip of the tail. You'll frighten it to death if you let it dangle, and besides that, the skin on its tail is so loose it might peel away. That's so painful for the little creature that then it might have to be destroyed."

"You sure know a lot about them," I complimented him.

Hank beamed. "You can try holding this one."

"No thanks," I said, probably a little too quickly. "It's very cute but I've got to get used to the idea that it's a pet and not something to be avoided in a back alley."

"I know what you're saying, but these are the friendliest little guys in the world if they're handled properly and not frightened."

"I'll try touching it for starters."

"Good idea. Just take one finger and gently stroke its fur."

I did exactly that, a bit gingerly, but I knew I had to overcome my reluctance to even get near it.

"Would you like to hold the mother? She's not so fragile" Hank asked.

"No thanks. I really should be getting home," I explained.

Hank looked disappointed, but I wasn't sure if it was because I didn't want to pick up the mother gerbil or because I told him I had to leave. I didn't want him to be annoyed with me so I said, "I'd really like to see you again . . . I mean them." I could feel myself blushing, because I hadn't meant to be so obvious, but Hank didn't seem to notice.

He put the baby gerbil back in the cage. Then he put his hands on my shoulders, looked me straight in the eye, and then seemed to sum me up. "I think there's hope for you. If you change your mind about wanting one or two for pets, I'll give you a couple of babies as soon as they're weaned. I have to separate them — that is, the boys from the girls — in about twenty days, or there'll be another litter. Then I'd have to quit school and go into the breeding business."

He was deadly serious, but I couldn't help laughing. "I'll have to ask my parents about whether I can start my own gerbil ménage." I was sure he could tell I was stalling, so to make sure he knew I was still interested I added, "But I'd love to visit you again . . . I mean visit the gerbils. They must grow very fast."

"You're right!" he exclaimed, as though this were the first intelligent remark I'd made all day. "Why don't you come over exactly one week from today? You'll see an enormous difference."

"It's a date," I agreed, thankful that I would see him again on a semi-social basis. And also, a week would give me time to read up on these funny fellows.

CHAPTER 28 _____

The rest of the week I devoted to learning about gerbils. I hoped to avoid Jeff in the library when I took some books out on the subject, but there was no way. I even tried to distract him while he was stamping them out, so that he might not notice the titles.

"Are you okay now?" I was referring to the fact that he'd been out with the flu.

"I'm fine." He looked at the titles of the books. "I see you're into gerbils. Planning to start a zoo, along with your basketball team and rock group?"

"What are you talking about?"

"You know." He sounded disgruntled, and of course I did know what he was talking about. There was nothing I could say, so I hurriedly took the books under my arms and left.

That night I plunged into my gerbil reading and crammed as much information as possible into my head. I forced myself to read the chapters on rodents in general, and look at the pictures. By the time I was ready to go to Hank's house again, supposedly to see what progress his little darlings had made, I was a walking gerbil encyclopedia. I was actually looking forward to spewing out my recently acquired knowledge.

We had arranged to meet just outside the school entrance as soon as the last bell rang. Actually, I hadn't seen Hank since "frog time" because lab meets only once a week, and the last time I'd had a different partner. Now, the minute I saw Hank, I couldn't wait to show off.

"You won't believe how much they've grown," Hank began as we strolled toward his house.

"Oh, I know. Newborn gerbils only measure about half an inch, don't have any teeth, are blind and deaf, and squeak a lot. At five or six days they measure about one inch."

"That's right." Hank looked rather amazed.

I took that as a sign of encouragement and continued rambling. "Mongolian gerbils, which are the kind generally sold as pets, accept handling when they're only a few days old. Lesser-known species resent human interference so much that they will kill and eat the whole litter."

"You've picked up a lot of information," Hank commented.

"I noticed you had a box of sunflower seeds next to their cage. That's very good, but did you know that they also thrive on canary seed, bread that has been soaked in milk, and fresh greens?"

"Hey, I thought *I* was teaching *you* about gerbils, not the other way around."

"You got me interested," I explained.

When we arrived at Hank's house, we went in the back door. Françoise, who was polishing silver over the sink, greeted us and immediately offered us some brownies she had baked. We each grabbed one and then headed for the cellar stairs.

"Don't tell me, Amy," Françoise called after me, "you want to see those furry things again."

"Can't wait," I told her, not quite honestly. But I was determined to fake my enthusiasm. As soon as we approached the cage, I exclaimed about how much they had grown.

"They're much bigger than the last time you were here," Hank said, "but I still can't tell them apart."

"That's because each new gerbil is a nearly exact replica of its parents."

"How'd ya know that?" Hank looked puzzled.

"If the parents are purebred, the baby will probably be exactly like its parents. The genes carry the inheritable characteristics — coat, color, eye color, texture of fur. Of the pair of genes it receives, that which shows itself in the young gerbil's appearance is known as the dominant gene."

"I suppose you memorized the Mendelian laws of heredity."

"Well, yes, I did happen to read about them." I was quite pleased that he could tell.

"Is there anything you don't know about gerbils? Anything I could tell you about?"

"Don't think so."

"I guess that ends the discussion." Hank seemed somewhat annoyed. Then he reached into the cage and pulled out one of the gerbils. "Are you ready for this?" he asked, shoving it toward me.

"Sure," I answered, tentatively holding out my hands.

He placed the creature on the palm of one of my hands, and I clapped my other hand over it to prevent it from falling.

"Be careful," he snapped. "You'll squeeze it to death."

I forced myself to relax my grip but couldn't hide my squeamishness.

"Take it easy," Hank instructed. "He's not going to bite."

"I know," I said nervously. "Gerbils only bite under exceptional circumstances, such as to protect themselves."

"You might just be one of those exceptions," Hank muttered. "Better give him to me."

Hank took him from me and let him lean on his shoulder.

"Whew," I sighed in relief.

"You really aren't ready to have them as pets yet," Hank observed.

"Guess not," I admitted.

"And it doesn't look as though I can teach you anything about gerbils that you don't already know."

"I'm still interested," I insisted.

"Really?" Hank looked at me suspiciously, as though he knew I wasn't telling the truth.

I watched in silence as he returned the gerbil to its cage. Then he straightened up and announced that he had to prepare a talk for the science club.

"It meets tomorrow, and I'm going to tell them about quarks."

"Quarks," I repeated.

"Never mind. I'm afraid if I get you started, I'll never hear the end of it."

"What do you mean?" I asked.

"Only kidding," he said. Then he put his hand on my shoulder and guided me up the stairs.

Françoise was no longer in the kitchen, so we were still alone. I desperately tried to think of something to say that would indicate to Hank that I wanted to see him again. The gerbils were no longer a good excuse, because he knew I didn't like them. Before I could come up with any other ideas, Hank offered me another brownie.

"Have one for the road," was the way he put it. He held the plate of brownies with one hand, and opened the back door with the other.

Not exactly subtle, I thought to myself. "No thanks," I muttered aloud. "I'm not a bit hungry."

"See you around," he said, as he held the door open for me.

" 'Bye," I mumbled without looking at him. I refused to let him see my face for fear he'd see how awful I felt.

I was more mad than sad — mad at myself, if I was to be perfectly honest, rather than sad about losing Hank. Not that I'd ever won him. But he was my last chance, my third failure; and it was less than two weeks until the prom.

CHAPTER 29 _____

The one comforting thought was that my family wasn't in on the gerbil phase of my life. I mean, it was fortunate that I hadn't gone so far as to set up housekeeping for some pets I would be responsible for the rest of their natural lives, or else put up for adoption. I could just imagine the flak I would have gotten from Kenny and Greg if I had gerbils for a week or two and then decided I didn't like them! In that respect, I had avoided a real disaster.

I tried not to talk about the prom with any members of my family, although I couldn't avoid the subject with my friends. Then one night at dinner, Kenny piped up with the information that his art teacher, Mr. Barry, had been asked by the decoration committee to come up with some original posters that could be hung on the gym walls for prom night.

"We've been working on this stuff for two weeks. I personally can't wait till it's over so I can get back to my wood carving," he complained.

"You've only got ten more days," Greg pointed out.

Then, as though it hadn't occurred to him before that second, Kenny squealed, "Hey, Amy, who you going with?"

"I'm not," I mumbled, trying to hold back the tears.

I could see my mother and father glance at each other and not say anything. That made me feel awful. Then, what really got me was Greg.

"You can always go with me. A bunch of kids from my class are going together."

"Go with my brother!" I wailed. I knew he meant well, but I could never live down that humiliation.

"Maybe we can do something special that night," my father suggested.

"Yeah, maybe we could see the Yankees play the Boston Red Sox," Kenny piped up.

"Or see *Annie* on Broadway," my mother said. "It's supposed to be great."

"Thanks," I muttered, knowing they were all trying to be nice, "but forget it."

"It's not the end of the world, Aim." My father's voice was sympathetic.

"I know," I sighed. But not for one moment did I believe it.

That night I cried myself to sleep, something I hadn't done since eighth grade when

I missed our end-of-the-year class picnic because I had a case of the mumps. Now that seemed insignificant compared to my present problem.

The next day was Friday, and since I didn't want to lie and make excuses and generally behave like a fink, I went to Rico's after school. I took my time getting there and I was still feeling like the pits, but I hoped it wouldn't show.

When I arrived, M.J. and Terry and Gail were already in a booth, talking. The minute I approached, they abruptly stopped and looked at me as though I'd caught them conspiring. M.J. was the first to recover and tried to sound her usual cheery self. "Sit down. We already brought you a Coke."

"Thanks," I said, still wondering why they all seemed so embarrassed.

Then Gail, out of thin air, began complaining about her brother and how she's tired of being a surrogate mother.

"What's that mean?" M.J. asked.

"It means I have to be in charge of him whenever my mother is working — which is three times a week."

"Teaches you responsibility," Terry kidded her.

"I have enough responsibility. Do you know what it's been like these past weeks getting everything ready for —"

Before she could finish her sentence, M.J. interrupted. "My problem is I don't have a little brother. Or sister. It's awful being an only child. Amy, aren't you glad you've got Kenny and Greg?"

"Sure," I answered tersely, not at all interested in getting into the conversation.

"My little sister's at the bratty stage, but I'm glad she's around," Terry admitted. "My parents are so busy getting her to shape up that the pressure's off me."

"You're lucky," M.J. commented. "I could do with less pressure."

The conversation went on around me about having siblings and being an only child and parental pressure, but I couldn't get involved. I'm not usually so quiet and it must have been obvious, but everyone was tactful enough not to ask me what was wrong. They already knew.

On the way home, even M.J., my best friend in the world, didn't mention my mood.

When I got to my house, I immediately trudged upstairs to my room so that I could be by myself for a few minutes. Then I realized what my friends had been talking about before I'd arrived at Rico's. They had decided not to mention the Junior Prom in front of me. Not only that: For the first time since I could remember, they hadn't even talked about boys!

I knew they had planned all that out of kindness, but somehow it only made me feel worse than ever. I was beginning to wonder if I'd ever feel good again.

CHAPTER 30 _____

I managed to get through the weekend, keeping busy every minute. My theory is that the only way to get out of the mental blahs is to be active. So I straightened my drawers, cleaned my closet, went bike-riding, watched TV, played scrabble with Greg, and volunteered to take Kenny and his friend Scott to see *Popeye* on Sunday afternoon.

None of this was enjoyable, but it had to be better than sulking. I hoped that I would feel better on Monday, but I seemed to be as distracted as ever — and always close to tears. I had trouble concentrating in class, and in history Mr. Newell — who looks like a young Burt Reynolds and who every girl in his class has a crush on, including me — shouted my name three times before I was aware that he was calling on me. If Molly, who was sitting next to me, hadn't tapped me on the shoulder, I'd probably still be sitting there. Then, of course, I didn't know the answer because I hadn't even heard the question. Mr. Newell just shook his head, muttering something about spring fever and called on someone else.

After school, I went to the library, convinced that I should go through the motions of a normal life. It was a bleak day, and no natural light poured into the usually sunny room. I sat down at my usual table at the far end of the room. There was no one around, and I felt more alone than I can ever remember.

I opened my math book to our assignment, but I couldn't focus on the problems. I turned to my history book, but the pages looked blurry and I gave up. I had tried not to dwell on the way I'd messed up my chances to get invited to the prom, but now I couldn't help remembering every detail.

Grant and Lenny and Hank — all three seemed to like me for a few hours, even a few days, and then they got turned off. It was hard to admit, but I knew I was so anxious to have them keep liking me that I changed myself — just to please them. And it always had the opposite effect.

I remembered how Grant had wanted to talk about Hemingway, and I had switched the subject to basketball. In fact, that was all I'd talked about the one night we'd gone out. And Lenny had loved the line I'd quoted to him — "music like a curve of gold." He'd even looked up the poem it came from, but I'd insisted after our first meeting to let him know how much I knew about guitar music. My last hope, Hank, I realized had loved teaching me. But I couldn't bear not showing him how much I knew about gerbils, when I couldn't care less. Even absentminded Hank could see through me.

Dumb, dumb, dumb, I thought. And then I couldn't hold back any longer. The tears that had been close to the surface for days streamed down my face.

I folded my arms on the table, buried my head in them, and couldn't stop sobbing. I don't know how long I stayed like that, but suddenly I felt a hand on my shoulder and a voice whispering, "Hey, what's wrong?"

I raised my head slightly and through blurry eyes recognized Jeff.

"Everything," I muttered, and brushed away my tears with the back of my hand.

"Here," Jeff said, digging in his pocket. "This is a perfectly clean handkerchief I reserve for damsels in distress." He shoved it in my hand and I wiped my face with it.

For some reason I didn't feel embarrassed. Maybe because my crying session was such a relief from all the tension that had been building up in me.

"Thanks for the hankie," I blubbered, and blew my nose.

"I bet I know what's wrong." Jeff looked serious.

"How would you know?" I asked.

"From the books you've been taking out."

"What do you mean?"

"I think you're having an identity crisis."

"A what?"

"You're trying to find out who you are — or else you're trying to be like someone else." Jeff explained.

"Why do you say that?" I was beginning to think Jeff knew everything.

"Because of the books you've been reading. You can tell a lot about people by the books they read."

"What's that make me?"

"Well, a while ago you were checking out basketball, the next thing you were into was guitar music, and just recently it was gerbils. I knew that wasn't what you really liked to read."

"You're right," I admitted.

"So if you weren't really interested for yourself, you must have been doing it for someone else."

Jeff was so close to the mark that it was spooky.

"I had a similar problem a year ago. Maybe it happens to everyone in the tenth grade."

"You sound like you're a hundred years older than I." I couldn't help smiling — the first time in days.

"It wasn't funny at the time. I almost had to leave home."

"What are you talking about?"

"It had to do with my father. I know he meant well, but for a while things were pretty hairy around our house."

161

"What did he want you to do?"

"It all started because he had always wanted to be a doctor. But his father died when he was a sophomore in college, and there was never enough money to send him to med school. In fact, he had to work part-time the last two years of college, and the idea of going to graduate school was out of the question."

"So he wanted you to be a doctor, since he never could be."

"Exactly. But that's the last thing in the world I want to be."

"And your mother?" Amy asked.

"My mother was on my side. She believes in doing your own thing."

"At least they weren't both against you."

"No, but there was an awful lot of tension in our house. I mean, my father would be completely silent at the dinner table. That was very unusual. For a while I even tried reading some medical books, thinking I might get interested. That would have solved everything."

"But it didn't work and you didn't give in."

"I couldn't. I knew I wanted to be a writer or an editor," Jeff said.

"So what'd ya do?"

"I told him the truth. I said I'd be a lousy doctor if I hated the field of medicine."

"And he said you were right?"

"Not right away. In fact he didn't say anything for about twenty-four hours, and then he told me I was right. I never felt so good in my life."

"Things were okay then?" Amy asked.

"Better than ever. My father even apologized for putting so much pressure on me."

"That's great," I said, realizing that this was the first time I had thought about anyone but myself.

Then the four-thirty bell rang and we both jumped. We had been so absorbed in talking that neither of us had realized how much time had passed.

Jeff stood up slowly and lowered his voice. "I'm supposed to finish stacking these books before closing time. Wait for me, though, and I'll walk you home. It's the least I can do after boring you with the story of my life."

"It wasn't a bit boring," I insisted. "But I'll wait for you anyway."

While Jeff stacked the books, I stared into space, thinking about whether I really did have an identity crisis. If I was honest, I told myself, I didn't have any problem at all knowing who I was — me, Amy, middle child, only daughter, favorite grandchild, who loved books, her family, her friends, the idea of love, volleyball, and getting good marks — not necessarily in that order.

So if it wasn't an identity crisis I was suffering from, it must be the other thing Jeff had mentioned — trying to be like someone else. That was more on target. I was thinking that I'd never let myself fall into that trap again when Jeff thrust a book under my nose.

"Read this," he instructed, pointing to a poem. "It's one of the books I was putting away. I dropped it, and when I picked it up it happened to turn to this page. It's a poem by Dorothy Parker."

I'll never know if Jeff had made up that story or if he really had dropped the book, but I'll always remember the poem he showed me.

It was about a woman who changed her ideas with each different man she went out with. Finally, she realizes she likes the way she is and now can say to men:

> "And if you do not like me so,
> To hell my love with you."

CHAPTER 31 ⸻⸻⸻⸻

At five o'clock the closing bell rang. I picked up my belongings and headed for the front desk where Jeff was clearing things away. I stood silently, waiting for him to finish.

"Not taking out any tomes on the ancient art of karate or how to build an igloo?" he asked.

For a moment I felt very defensive, but Jeff was grinning so contagiously that I had to smile back.

"Nope," I answered, "I don't happen to know any black belts or Eskimos."

Jeff laughed out loud and said, "I'll be right with you. I just have to get my jacket."

When he came back from the closet, which was next to the door, he brushed right past me.

"Wrong way," I told him.

"No it's not," he called back. "I want to

get you a book that's just come out. It's a page-turner and well written besides."

"Great," I remarked, thinking that I hadn't had time to read for pleasure for months.

When he came back with the book and handed it to me, I asked. "What's it about?"

"It's about a girl who knows she's adopted. She's very unhappy and thinks if she finds her natural parents, everything will be all right."

"And does she?"

"I'm not going to tell. That would spoil it for you."

Jeff took one last look at the checkout desk. "That should pass Kruger's inspection. She's nice but she's too neat. She had to leave early tonight and told me to put everything away."

"Looks perfect," I remarked.

"Always do what I'm told." Jeff smiled at me sideways, and I couldn't help thinking how cute he was. Also, for the first time, he had talked about himself. Was it because he'd caught me in such a weakened condition that he was able to loosen up? Was it his tactful way of getting me to feel better? Whatever the reason, he'd succeeded in getting me to stop thinking about myself.

On the way home, Jeff kept talking about books. I was so riveted by what he was saying that I was looking at him rather than in front of me when we came to a stop street. A car was making a turn in front of us and I would have plunged right ahead if Jeff hadn't had very quick reflexes. I was just about to smack into it when Jeff grabbed my arm with both hands and pulled me back into the curb.

"Watch it, kiddo," the man behind the wheel yelled, and sped off.

"Close call," I breathed. "I think you just saved my life, Jeff."

"My good deed for the day." He was smiling, and he hadn't let go of my arm.

"Your second good deed. I might have started a flood in the library if you hadn't loaned me your handkerchief."

"That was nothing, compared to saving your life."

Just another form of lifesaving, I thought, but I didn't say it out loud.

He casually slid his hand down my arm and took my hand. He gave my hand a significant squeeze as he took a look up and down the street.

"Is it safe to cross?"

"Just follow me," he ordered, taking a step off the curb.

To the ends of the earth, I thought.

CHAPTER 32 ⎯⎯⎯⎯⎯⎯

The rest of the way home we talked about books. Jeff told me about John Knowles's latest.

"It's called *Peace Breaks Out*. All about life in a New England prep school."

"I loved *A Separate Peace*. It really knocked me out."

"This one has the same setting — Devon School in New Hampshire. All those rolling hills and wholesome kids."

"Except they're not."

"Of course not. They're motivated by jealousy, and a need to excel — at any price. Even the good guys get involved in settling scores."

"I bet it ends in tragedy."

"If I tell you the ending, you might not bother to read it."

"I might not, but I know for sure I'll read it if you *don't* tell me the ending."

We had arrived at my house, and at the same time we'd run out of conversation. I stood at my door, facing him, reluctant to say good-bye. I thought of inviting him in, but it was one of the nights I had to get dinner ready.

"Well," I muttered, as I reached in my bag for my key.

"Well," Jeff echoed. He was staring hard at his shoes, as though they might be sending him messages.

I thought of saying thank you again, but he'd be embarrassed and so would I.

"I'll wash and iron your handkerchief tonight, and bring it back to you tomorrow." I was really groping for something to say.

"Keep it," he said. "I've got eleven others just like them at home." He glanced at me quickly and smiled, and then went back to staring at his shoes. He didn't seem to want to leave either.

"Eleven others!" I exclaimed.

"They come by the dozen," he explained.

"Oh, I see." I nodded my head in understanding as though he'd just made clear Einstein's theory of relativity.

We stood there in silence another minute, and then I turned to open the door.

"I'd like to see you again, Amy," Jeff mumbled rapidly.

"Me too, Jeff. That is, I'd like to see you again."

"I mean, not just in the library."

"That's what I mean." I faced him again,

but he was back to staring at his shoes. Then he took a deep breath and raised his head so that he was looking right at me.

"Would you like to go to the Junior Prom with me?" he asked.

I hadn't thought about the prom for at least an hour, and I was in a state of shock. Literally speechless.

Jeff looked crestfallen, and then mumbled something about how he was probably too late asking. "See you around," he said, tonelessly, and started to back away.

"Wait," I breathed. "Did I hear you ask me about the prom?"

"Yeah, but I guess I'm too late."

"You're not. You're right on time."

"I am?" He stopped cold in his tracks and his face lit up.

"I'd love to go with you." It wasn't easy to keep my voice normal, I was so excited.

"I can't believe it." Jeff ran forward and threw his arms around me.

"Me neither," I said, not quite sure what I meant. I started to say something else, but Jeff still had me in his arms, and then I felt his lips press against mine.

When he finally let me go I couldn't speak, even if I'd wanted to. I guess he felt the same, because he backed away slowly, not taking his eyes off me. I stood frozen to the spot, watching him until he disappeared down the block, and I still didn't move. I don't know how long I stayed in one position.

I'd forgotten that I'd partly opened the

door to our house, when I suddenly heard Kenny's voice behind me.

"Amy," he squealed, "you're letting all the cold air in, you're supposed to be fixing dinner, and I'm stuck on my homework."

"Uh, huh," I replied, dreamily.

"Amy, do you know what you're doing?"

"For the first time in a long time," I answered.

RELATIONSHIPS...FRIENDS...
BOYFRIENDS...IT'S INTENSE...
IT'S BEING A TEENAGER... ?

IT'S
TOTALLY HOT!
THE WILD NEW SERIES!

Experience the ups and downs in the lives of **Miranda, Kat, Eric, Brent,** and other guys and girls who feel just like you—that relationships and being a teenager just don't come easy!

Don't miss these TOTALLY HOT! books

❏ BAC44560-X	#1	**Losing Control**	$2.95
❏ BAC44561-X	#2	**Breaking Away**	$2.95
❏ BAC44562-6	#3	**Standing Alone**	$2.95
❏ BAC44563-4	#4	**Making Changes**	$2.95

Available wherever you buy books, or use this order form.

- -